Jackson Red Horne

Volume One

Dead Men Walking

- J. K. Hulon -

ISBN 978-1480152687

To The Old Man
& My Jenny

Sunday

05:49

Petra Wilson awoke with a bang.

Whether the noise was real or just an auditory echo left over from the dream she was having, she didn't know. She didn't really care. As she settled back into her pillow, Petra was just glad to be awake. She loathed sleeping. She only did it because her body required it.

After a few minutes, she rolled over to look at the clock- it was already almost six. She uttered a curse, but didn't get up just yet. She dropped her head back into the pillow, grinding her palms into her eyes.

Usually, she was up and moving by five thirty, but last night had been rough. Even though she kept no calendars in the house, she knew that today was the day, ten years ago, when Father Richard and those two men in Army green knocked on her door.

That old saw about time healing all wounds was pure horse apples. For Petra, the feelings of

1

loss and grief were as bad now as they ever were.

Ignoring the calendar in her head and the desire to just collapse into her misery, she rolled out of bed, wrapping herself in her dead husband's robe and made her way into the kitchen.

She put on the coffee, lighting her first cigarette of the day with the flame from the stove. She inhaled deeply as the pot popped and the water began to warm. She exhaled a long stream of smoke before reaching into the cabinet for two mugs.

Every Sunday morning since the war ended, her brother, the honorable Sheriff Ben Hoyle, stopped by on his way to church to drop off the paper. They'd share a cup of coffee and a smoke while making small talk.

She didn't mind the company even if she didn't really care for her brother. He'd been there when her husband was shot through the head by a German sniper- the visits were sort of an act of penance for Ben, but Petra found them more patronizing than anything else. Elections were always right around the corner and caring for a war widow tended to help with the votes.

The clock on the wall said it was now quarter of six. The coffee was ready, but Ben wasn't there yet. As a child, he had always been late-school, chores, jobs, dates; anytime Ben needed to be somewhere, he wasn't. After Pearl was

2

bombed, Ben enlisted in the Army and Petra's little brother transformed into a disciple of routine. These days, he was punctual to a fault, taking pride in it, boasting about it. And if something came up, if his schedule changed, even by a matter of a minute or two, he always called. It got annoying sometimes.

By six thirty, an angry black cloud hung over Petra's head. She didn't have much of anything to do that day, church, a few household chores and an errand or two to run in town, but she preferred to get these weekly visits with Ben over with and out of the way as quickly as possible.

At six forty five, she dropped her third cigarette of the morning into her brother's cold cup of coffee and got up from the table. She just knew that as soon as she stepped into the shower, her brother would be ringing the doorbell. If Ben wasn't going to call and explain his tardiness, Petra would call him. She strode into the living room, her robe flowing behind her like a tyrant's cape. As she reached for the phone, riot act in hand, a soft scraping noise caught her attention. It sounded like someone lightly dragging their fingernails down the screen door.

Muttering the harshest explicatives a good church going woman could think of, Petra strode through the living room. She was in no mood for pranks.

"Damn you, Benjamin, if you think this is funny, you've got another think coming!" she barked, yanking the front door open.

Her scream was loud enough to wake the neighbors a quarter mile down the road.

Ben Hoyle stood on the doorstep, poking at random points on the door frame, trying to find the button for the doorbell. He was having a hard time of it, what with the three inch hole burned through the center of his face.

Petra could see the neighbor's windmill through her brother's head.

The bell rang just as Petra hit the floor.

The sun had been up for more than an hour before Red stirred in the back seat of his '53 Mercury Monterey. He scrubbed the stubble of his beard, rubbing his eyes. The girl lying on top of him clucked softly then began snoring again. Sliding out from under her, he slipped over into the front seat. Digging in the glove box, he found one of his cigars and pushed the lighter into the dash. Yawning deep enough to make his neck pop, Red ran a hand through his jet black hair while waiting for the lighter to warm up. He ran his tongue over his teeth- they felt furry.

A cigar wouldn't help at all.

It was probably a good thing then that the lighter wasn't working. Red checked the ignition, remembering he'd left the radio on last night while he and his lady friend had had a good time.

He was just about to step out of the car and look for someone to give him a jump start when he realized he was as naked as the day he was born.

He'd picked up the girl down at The Barn- a local watering hole that had once been a fishing camp at the base of the Sego River Falls. It was a real dive, but no worse than some of the other places he'd been in around the world. The girl had been waiting tables, completely immune to the charms of the roughnecks, cowboys, and military men that frequented the joint. But for whatever reason, she just melted when Red turned on the charm. When the last of the drunks slouched out the door, Red offered the girl a ride home. But when they got to his car, she had other ideas.

He'd only planned on a little necking, but she was more than willing and Red was definitely able.

She got what she wanted. Red got more than he needed and following a sweaty hour and a half in the back seat of the Mercury, the girl finally gave up what Red was really after...

Information.

After killing three people during the commission of a bank robbery, the girl's brother had gone to ground in Big Wells. And now Captain Andrew Jackson 'Red' Horne, Texas Ranger would bring Wesley Cooper to justice.

Red hooked an arm over into the backseat, reaching for his pants, just in time to hear the girl slamming the door shut. She was naked as a jay bird, running towards a faded green pickup truck, Red's clothes and boots bundled in her arms.

Three men had stepped out of the old Chevy and were walking towards the Mercury. One had a bat, another had a rope, and the third- Red recognized him as Wes Cooper- cradled a Thompson machine gun in his arms.

The girl had set him up.

Red savagely swore to himself. His badge and gun were locked in the trunk under the spare tire. He'd been undercover for three weeks, not expecting to make an arrest this soon.

Naked as the day he was born, Red got out of the car...

Nothing to do but to get to it.

"Wesley Cooper, you are under arrest for robbery and murder. Put down your weapon and come along peaceably."

The men stopped about ten feet from Red. All three were laughing, Cooper the loudest.

"You've got some balls. That's pretty obvious. But we've got you, three to one. So unless you can shoot lead from your pecker, you're going to die here."

Red shook his head, "I'm the only one here with my dick out, but you're the ones pulling your puds. If you're going to throw down, let's do it."

The bat man leapt forward, club raised high over his head. Before he could swing it down on Red's skull, the Ranger ducked under his swing, catching the bat in his left hand and driving his right fist into the man's abdomen. Using his opponent's momentum against him, Red flipped the man over his shoulder. The bat man grunted as he hit the ground, flat on his back, the wind knocked out of his lungs. Red plucked the club out of his limp hands as the rope man came at him from behind.

He got the cord around Red's neck, but the Ranger was quicker. He slid a forearm between the rope and his throat, easily ripping the hemp out of the other man's grip- the fool had it looped over itself too many times to get a good hold on it. And the bat made a satisfying *thok* against the man's head, dropping him like a load of bricks.

While Red was dealing with his two accomplices, Cooper had gotten tangled in the Thompson's sling. He was still trying to get the gun up to his shoulder when Red planted the ash club in his groin. Cooper dropped the Thompson and bent over, clutching his balls. Red cracked the bat across his back, sending Cooper into the dirt, completely knocking the fight out of him before he could even begin.

Red threw the bat to the side, striding across the parking lot towards the girl in the truck, her eyes wild as she fumbled with the ignition keys. Just as Red was reaching for the door handle the Chevy roared to life. The girl dropped the truck in gear and sped off in a cloud of caliche dust.

All Red could do was stand there, swearing as his clothes drove off.

"Damn."

Chief Deputy Buck Wyndell stood over the body of his boss, wondering just how in the hell to move forward.

It's not every day there's a murder in Hoyle County. Death itself was common out here: snake bite, a drowning or two during the spring floods, tractor roll-overs during the harvest, a random lightning strike during the summer thunderstorms, old age- Buck had seen them all during the sixty two years he had walked the earth. But staring at the body of his boss, a good friend and a good man, lying face down with a hole big enough to park a truck in burned through the head is a little unsettling.

And the dandelion that had popped up through the wound was a coda Buck could do without.

He leaned over and plucked the weed. After a moment's contemplation, the Chief Deputy blew the fluff to the four winds, hoping they would carry his wish to the powers that be. He turned to find one of the other deputies staring at him.

"What? Every little bit helps."

Deputy John Haby shrugged and walked up to the house. The other two county deputies- Bert and Joe Tom Harris were on the porch with the Sheriff's sister. Miss Petra was drifting in and out of consciousness- it had been quite a shock, opening the door to find her brother walking around on the porch in his current state.

Buck took his hat off, wiping his brow with his sleeve. He thumped his finger against the face of his wrist watch, not believing it was only 8:30 in the morning. The heat was already climbing through the nineties and if the coroner didn't get here soon, things were going to get really ripe really quick.

He was kind of surprised that it hadn't already.

Just as Buck was hollering for a deputy to give Frank Angstrom's office another call, the physician pulled up in his old Pontiac.

The doctor struggled to extricate himself from the sedan, nearly slipping in the loose gravel of the driveway. If he went down, it was a sure bet the doc would need the help of three men to get up again. Much to Buck's relief, the doctor gained some sense of stability, hitched his pants and waddled up the driveway.

To say Frank had a weight problem was the understatement of the decade. Years of pecan pie coupled with a sedentary lifestyle had done a number on Frank's waistline. Sweating buckets and grunting like a pig, he made his way over to Buck and the Sheriff's body as quickly as his stubby legs could carry him. How the man managed to avoid a full-blown heart attack on a daily basis, Buck would never know.

"Jesus Christ, Buck... what in the Hell happened here?" Frank grimaced as he looked over the body. "I can see his damn brains in there!"

"Hullo, Frank. If you would, please, let's just get down to business here. Declare him dead so we can get him out of here."

"All right, all right." Frank waddled over to the other side of body and tried to get down on his knees without falling over- Buck would have laughed at the effort any other time. Halfway down, the doc gave up, wiping the sweat off his face with the back of his hand. The doc rummaged through his black bag and handed Buck a thermometer. "Stick this in him like you would your wife's pot roast."

"Oh Good Lord, Frank!" Buck threw the thermometer back at the doctor.

"How am I going to know time of death if I don't get his liver temp?"

Buck massaged his temples, gritting his teeth. He'd known Frank for nearly thirty years-the man was not squeamish in the least, but he had no real people skills when it came to shit like this.

"He's been laying here since he fell over and stopped moving at a quarter to seven this morning." Buck sighed as heavy a sigh as any man in history could only ever dream of sighing. "Why don't you go check on Mrs. Wilson, Frank? She hit her head pretty hard when she found her brother out here. She's been delirious and rambling since we found her."

"What about the Sheriff?" Frank continued to perspire, fidgeting with the thermometer.

"Just declare him dead. We need to get him out of here before it gets really hot. You can stick your thermometer in him all you want back at the office."

"All right, all right, no need to get in a huff. I hereby declare the sheriff to be dead. Happy?"

Buck bit his tongue. "Just go check on Petra, please. Thank you."

Frank shrugged and started to the house.

"And Doc," Buck added, "try to *not* be you for a few minutes."

The Chief Deputy watched the doctor struggle up the steps of the porch. The deputies weren't sure who was in need of more assistance- the sheriff's sister or the doctor. It would have been funny, except for the dead body lying in the grass at Buck's feet. When they finally made it inside, Buck turned his attention back to Ben Hoyle's earthly remains.

He was just about to roll the body over when he heard a commotion behind him. Buck turned to look, but had a hard time comprehending what he was seeing.

Three men, battered, bruised and naked but for dirty white skivvies, were tied together at the ankles like a prison chain gang. A fourth man with Tommy gun rode herd on the motley crew. Calling out for one of the deputies in the house, Buck started towards the group.

He knew two of men pretty well, Del Wheaton and Jorge Zavala- local ne'er-do-wells that had spent more than a few days in the county lock up. It was never anything serious, usually drunk and disorderly on pay day. The third man might have been little Dizzy Cooper's older brother, but Buck hadn't seen Wes in probably ten years. The bruises and swelling made it hard to tell.

The fourth man looked vaguely familiar, but Buck wasn't entirely certain of his identity. None of his clothes fit right and his long black hair hung down in his face. But the man carried himself and the machine gun with utter authority.

Buck pushed his hat back on his head and leaned his arms on the white rail fence. The man with the machine gun gave a jerk on the rope, halting his prisoners. When the he pulled his black hair away from his face, Buck got a good look at the man's red handlebar mustache.

"Hullo, Red, long time, no see." Buck offered the Ranger a handshake. "You look like hell, son."

"Buck," Red acknowledged the deputy with a firm grip and a wry smile. "It's been a busy morning."

"Hey there, Del... Jorge... How's it going?"

The men shuffled their feet in the dirt.

"Hey, Buck. It's going alright, I guess," Del spoke up. The side of his head was purple and he was having a hard time focusing with the one eye that wasn't swollen shut.

"We done screwed up this time, Buck," Jorge added. He looked like he had been throwing up.

"You got that right," Buck replied, fishing a mostly empty pack of smokes out of his shirt pocket. He put one to his lips while offering one to Red. The Ranger took it and accepted a light.

Tucking the pack of smokes in his breast pocket, Buck turned to Red's prisoners. "You

13

boys are dumber than a sack of hammers, trying to take on a Texas Ranger all by yourselves."

"Mr. Cooper there killed some men while robbing a bank in San Antonio. These two numbskulls thought it would be a good idea to help hide him out until the heat died down. One accomplice got away this morning. I'll have to track her down later."

"Let me guess… Dizzy Cooper," Buck chuckled as Red nodded his head. "You might have bitten off more than you can chew with that one, son. She's hotter than a two dollar pistol and can wiggle her hips better than any gypsy belly dancer, but she is twice as poisonous as any copperhead."

"Like I said, it's been a busy morning," Red flicked the ashes of his cigarette. "It looks like you're having a pretty full day as well." Red nodded towards to the body in the yard.

"Yep," Buck took his hat off, wiping more sweat from his balding scalp, damn this heat. "Sheriff's been murdered."

"Ben Hoyle?"

Buck nodded, "Somebody blew hole clean through his head. And I do mean clean. No blood, bone, or brain matter anywhere."

Red told his prisoners to sit and they collapsed in a heap on the side of the road. Sling the Tommy gun over his shoulder, Red went through the gate into the yard.

"I'm guessing you already called the district office?"

"Yep. I was surprised as Hell when they said they were going to send *you* over after you got around to checking in this morning."

"Why the surprise?"

"You may not realize it yet, but a lot of people round here were starting to think you were dead. It's been what... two, three years? You might oughta know some of your kinfolk started the paperwork to have you declared dead about six weeks ago. I wouldn't let the judge sign off on 'em, though. I had a feeling you'd turn up sooner or later."

Red's face hardened a bit, but didn't dwell on the thought.

"I appreciate that Buck. I just got back last month and didn't have time to shave or get a haircut even before the boys in Austin sent me down into the Valley, looking for that reprobate," Red jerked a thumb towards Wesley Cooper. "I haven't had a chance yet to call HQ this morning- we just happened to be walking by here on our way into Six Guns." Red took a long, last drag off the cigarette and crushed it under his heel. "I do need to let them know I've made contact with you and get 'em down here to pick up those three. And if ain't too much trouble, I'd appreciate if someone could tow my car in from down by the river- battery's flat."

"Petra's got a phone inside. I'll get Deputy Haby to call San Antonio back. The Harris twins can take your prisoners over to the office an' hold them until a wagon can get down here."

"Much appreciated, Buck."

"And when we get a minute, you probably ought to call your family and let them know you're alive."

"I'll take care of that later. Let's have a look at the Sheriff." Red turned to the three men sitting by the road. "Play nice with the deputies when they get out here, or else."

Wesley Cooper raised his head. "Or else what?" he whistled through his broken teeth.

"Or else I'll be very upset." Red pointed a finger at the man. "So far, you've only seen me being nice. Let your imagination run a little wild with that."

Red turned back to Buck and gave the Chief Deputy a wink.

The two men walked over to the lifeless corpse lying in the yard. Red squatted down besides the body and examined the hole.

"You ever see anything like this?" Buck asked, still having a hard time holding back his bile every time he looked at the Sheriff's remains.

"Actually... I have," Red answered, clearly shaken.

"Really?" Buck exclaimed.

A heartbeat later the Ranger checked himself, "Hell no. This is a new one on me." Red lied, gently rolling the body over on its back. The hole was perfect- three inches in diameter, centered right between the eyes, bloodless. Even the eye balls had been cleanly cauterized. Just like the wound he'd seen on that man, seven months ago, in Shanghai.

"He was sitting in his patrol car when it happened," Buck said, pointing to the Ford parked in the road, past the driveway. "For some reason he stopped in the road, fired one round from his pistol, into the dirt, not sure if that was before or after he was shot through the head." Buck paused for a minute, trying to maintain some sense of composure. "Whatever it was that did this to Ben's head also punched a hole clean through car's glass. How he walked to the front door and rang the bell, I just don't know."

Red judged the distance from the vehicle to the front door of the ranch house as nearly fifty yards. From the door back to the middle of the front lawn was another 20 yards. Red had seen men with more brain matter blown away walk just as far before they realized they were dead, but he still had a hard time believing it. He looked down at the body again and noticed something folded up and tucked under the sheriff's badge- a worn and faded photograph.

Red pulled the picture out and unfolded it. He showed it to Buck. "Recognize any of these men?"

"That's Ben Hoyle, of course," Buck pointed to the man in the middle of the photo. "On his left is Anthony Paxton. The man on the right is Eddie Cork. The one next to him is Lucas Brown."

"Lucas Brown…" Red turned the name over in his head for a second, "*Luke* Brown, owner of Brown Coastal and Refining?"

"Yeah, that's him. Nice enough guy, if you like cut throat bastards. I've had dinner with him more than once, over at Ben's house."

"I've met him before. About three years ago I was working a case down in Galveston. Some shrimpers tried to sink an oil rig belonging to the company he was working for at the time. I spent a weekend running and gunning with the man but had no idea he had any ties out here." Red pointed to the fifth man in the photograph. "What about this guy? You recognize him?"

"I have never seen that guy. Which is odd," Buck took the picture from Red, turning it over in his hands. He held it up to the sun, studying it, "because I've seen this picture, this exact same photograph, more times than I can count. But that man," the Chief Deputy tapped his finger on the man to the far right, "he is not in it."

Red took the photo back from Buck and examined it more closely. It was a standard Kodak print, 'Property US Army' stamped on the back, dated December 18, 1945- over nine and a half years ago. The five men were in civvies, submachine guns slung around their necks, arms around each other's shoulders, smiling. Red couldn't tell where they were, it looked like the flight line of an airfield, somewhere in the Pacific maybe.

"Where'd you see this other version?"

"On the mantle, over the fireplace in Ben's home. A bigger copy, eight by ten in a nice frame…"

Red covered the fifth man with his thumb, but Buck shook his head.

"The picture wasn't cropped, it was doctored. That man does not exist in the copy I've seen."

Tucking the picture into his shirt pocket, Red got to his feet.

"Maybe we ought to head over to Hoyle's house and take a look at that other copy. Poke around a bit. He married? Got any kids?"

"Just the wife, Marlene. Nobody's called her yet."

The two men were turning to go when the town's emergency siren started up. They looked toward the horizon, for the first time noticing the column of black smoke rising into the sky.

Two pumper trucks were blocking the street in front of the fire, engines idling. A few volunteer firemen stood in a small, frustrated group while the house burned to the ground. Buck uttered a fiery epithet, jumping out of the cruiser so quick that Red had to reach over and pull the parking brake himself. One of the firemen came running up to meet Buck in the middle of road. Red caught up with them and the cause of Buck's distress became obvious.

"That's the Sheriff's house. And there is no goddamn water," Buck took his hat off, slamming it on the ground.

Red shook his head, leaving Buck to mobilize the volunteers. He focused his attention on the crowd that had gathered for the show.

About a dozen housewives stood on the sidewalk of the oak lined street, whispering to each other behind their hands. The few men that were standing around appeared to be retired military- they congregated in a small group apart from the gossips, arms crossed over their chests, exchanging only a few brief words now and again. Red took immediate notice of a pair of men apart from the crowds, watching from about three houses down across the street. Blue jeans, white shirtsleeves, crew cuts, probably active duty, but before Red could get Buck's attention and point them out, a cloud of smoke drifted between them and the Ranger. When the light breeze cleared the air, the men had vanished.

The Chief Deputy was in a heated discussion with one of the fire fighters. Upon tapping the first hydrant, the flow had been good for about ten, maybe fifteen minutes, but then the water turned muddy brown and the pressure dropped to nothing. The recent and persistent drought had most likely caused the ground to buckle, shifting a pipe, breaking the main somewhere along the line. The Six Guns South VFD didn't have their own tanker, just a pumper and two equipment haulers. Buck was in the process of requesting a couple of tankers from Iron Mesa AFB as Red walked over to the small crowd of women across the street.

After convincing them that in spite of the ill-fitting filthy clothes, the long hair, and the unkempt beard, he was indeed a Texas Ranger, Red found that none of them had seen anything useful. Most of them had been inside when they heard the sirens. The rest had been out in their backyards, tending their gardens. None of them had been the one to call it in. But they all had something to say about the Sheriff, or rather, the Sheriff's wife…

Most, if not all of them, were convinced that Marlene Hoyle was having an affair with someone. At odd hours of the day, there were often strange cars parked in front of the house, men in black suits that never waved to the neighbors. To Red, they sounded more like government officials than anything else.

Red deduced the accusations against Marlene more than likely stemmed from her pedigree than anything else...

She was from out of town, don't you know? Why couldn't Ben marry a local girl?

Red could barely keep from rolling his eyes, but he was able to maintain a polite demeanor throughout the interview. He would have asked them about the men he'd seen a few houses down, but the description fit just about every able bodied man in town- this was a military community, after all; had been for decades. Red kept looking over the ladies' heads, scanning the sidewalks as they went on about men in black suits and quilting bees and damned Yankee interlopers, but the men with the crew cuts and shirtsleeves never showed themselves again.

Thanking them for their time, Red left them with something more to talk than just the Ben Hoyle's wife- a Texas Ranger was investigating the fire at the Sheriff's house and the Sheriff was nowhere to be seen. (Red didn't mention the Sheriff's murder. Someone else could kick over that can of worms.) Red briefly contemplated going over to talk to the men standing apart from their wives, but more than likely the only reason they were out here was that they had been dragged them away from their morning papers by their women when the sirens went off.

When the pumper trucks from the air force base showed up, Red offered to help with the firefighting effort. He was honestly relieved when the firefighters insisted they had it under control. Red hadn't done any firefighting since boot camp, more than ten years ago. It was a rush, to be sure, but one Red preferred to not experience again anytime soon.

Leaning up against the patrol car, Red went to steal a cigarette from the pack on the dashboard, but the empty pack. Red crumpled it up and tossed it through the open window onto the seat. He checked his watch, figuring it would be at least noon before they could shift through the debris. Red waited for Buck to slow down a minute and then got his attention.

"Hey, I'm taking the car. I want to check on a few things while you're knocking this down." Actually, Red just wanted to get out of these rancid clothes and back into uniform. And to see if maybe he could catch sight of the men he'd seen standing apart from the crowd earlier.

"Yeah, go on." Buck fished the keys out of his pockets, tossing them to Red. "Pick me up a new pack of Camels on your way back."

Red gave him quick two fingered salute, firing up the Ford. But before heading over to the cheap motel he was staying in, Red did a quick circle around the block. He saw no sign of the fellows with the crew cuts.

Probably nothing, Red thought to himself, turning onto Main Street.

Buck had just finished loading the hoses onto the back of the second pumper truck when his Ford rolled up.

Buck did a double take when Red got out of the car. The Ranger was dressed in what he called his uniform- a long sleeved khaki shirt with a black tie, crisp blue jeans, cowboy boots, and a grey Stetson. His long black hair was now closely cropped and the scraggily beard was trimmed away from the neat handlebar mustache. Instead of the customary revolver, Red wore a 1911 in a low slung cowboy holster.

"You're making me look bad, Red," Buck said, wiping soot across his forehead with the back of his hand.

"Yeah, well, wearing the clothes of three men who obviously hadn't bathed in over a week was getting to be too much."

Buck dismissed Red's explanation with the wave of a hand. "Don't worry, son. You're about to get dirty again. Let's see what we can find in this mess."

They carefully picked their way through the smoking ruin of the Sheriff's home. The intensity of the inferno had reduced the one-story brick ranch to a smoldering, roofless shell filled with smoking ash and charred timbers. About all they were going to find was ruin.

A house fire has a very distinct smell compared to a brush fire or a burning pile of leaves- a thin hazy fog of smoke reeking of burnt wood, scorched drywall, melted insulation, and soot-filled water. The smell was pervasive and intense.

Red had always considered that smell to be the soul of the house itself scorched by the flames.

Surveying the remains, Red doubted that the outcome would have been any different if the hydrants had been working from the start. Of the interior walls, a few studs burned down to ragged spikes were all that remained. The roof had collapsed and mostly burned away. Every piece of furniture and every personal item inside the house had been reduced to ash.

There were only two chances of finding any clues here: Slim and none.

Following the burn patterns, Red wandered over to the back of the house, near the back door, in what used to be the kitchen. Red was not an expert, but he'd investigated more than a few arsons over the years. It was obvious to him that this was where the inferno had started. Most house fires did start in the kitchen- a skillet full of grease, a towel to close to a burner and everything a person has accumulated in life goes up in flames. But as Red poked around, an odd contraption caught his eye- a couple of burnt and ruptured tanks on some sort of rack lay in the ashy muck. He dug through the debris and found the rest of the device.

It was a flamethrower.

Red had seen enough of them while fighting his way across the Pacific, but this one wasn't standard Government Issue. It looked homemade. The tanks were smaller than normal, the user would probably only get one or two good bursts and then be done. In Red's opinion, a setup like only had one purpose...

He continued searching through the remains of the kitchen and gave a start as he flipped over a piece of plywood covered with shingles. Buck hurried over, sliding to a stop, cursing and crossing himself for the first time in five years.

The body of Marlene Hoyle lay in the debris. All her clothes and hair had been burned off, but her skin was flawless, save for a slight blue tint, some ashen smudges, and a three inch hole burned through her heart. Her eyes were open, staring up into the sky with a crystal-clear gaze.

"Sweet Jesus, Mary Mother of God..." Buck clutched his chest. Even after forty four years on the job, his ticker couldn't take this kind of shock without stumbling through a few beats. Steadying the chief deputy, Red walked him out of the rubble into the back yard. Buck slumped up against a tree trunk, his breathing rapid and shallow.

"You gonna be all right?"

Buck breathed deep, fighting down hyperventilation. "I'll be fine. I just... damn..."

A few retirees who had lingered after the trucks had left were standing in the alley and witnessed the Chief Deputy's distress. A retired Army captain named Bob Pepper quickly came

26

over with a can of beer and one of his own nitroglycerin tablets. Buck thanked the man, chasing the pill with a sip of lager. Red the deputy's shoulder a pat.

"You sit here a spell. I'll go back in and check on the body," Red turned to Bob. "Could you get the one of the deputies over here? And tell them to make sure Frank Angstrom is on his way."

The older man gave a quick nod and went around to the front of the house. Red took a deep breath and walked back into the debris.

In spite of what he'd told Buck, Red avoided the body- that could wait for Frank. He knew the doctor had absolutely no problem with death, whatever bizarre form it had decided to take. He poked around in the rest of the rubble, a pointless venture he thought, until he found the door.

Underneath a few charred timbers, next to what was left of the refrigerator was a heavy steel plate, set in the slab. Storm cellars and bomb shelters were somewhat common out here, but to Red's eye, this looked more like the entrance to a heavy bunker. He cleared away the ashes and smoking wood with his boot, searching for the handle.

Red found an iron ring recessed in the door and gave it a yank. He was expecting more resistance, but the hatch flew open easily, throwing the Ranger off his balance. It was engineered with a very sophisticated counterweight system- too sophisticated for a simple storm cellar. Concrete steps lead down

27

through a dim, white-washed stairwell. Hundreds of gallons of water from the firefighting effort had flowed through the seams around the door, but Red could hear the sound of water trickling down a drain from somewhere below.

As Red put his foot on the first step, someone put a hand on his shoulder. The Ranger nearly jumped out of his skin, spinning around, slapping the butt of his 1911.

"You're kind of jumpy for a Texas Ranger," Buck gave Red a wink and held out a flashlight.

"Jesus H. Christ, Buck. You damn near gave *me* a heart attack. Are you trying to get shot?" Red swiped the flashlight out of the chief deputy's hand. "I take it you're all better now?"

"Those nitro pills work pretty damned quick," Buck was still grinning. Red gave him a hard look and turned back to the stairs.

Together they went down into the Sheriff's hidden vault.

Red counted the steps as they went down. They curved slightly to the left, ending at fifty one- about three stories underground. The room at the bottom was spacious, fifty feet by fifty feet, and brick lined; the walls, ceiling and floor painted white. About an inch of water covered the stone floor but it appeared to rapidly draining somewhere. A desk and chair occupied one corner, along with a tall file cabinet and a massive safe. A large corkboard covered the wall opposite the desk. Photographs, newspaper clippings, and hand written notes were pinned to every square inch.

Opposite the stairs leading down from the house were two more flights- one climbing back up, the other leading down.

"I have been in Ben Hoyle's house hundreds of times and I never knew this existed…" Buck said, not without a twinge of fear and a touch of awe. Red thought he heard a little bit of self-reproach in the man's voice.

"Every man has a secret life, Buck. You, me, Ben Hoyle," Red played his flashlight across the wall. "Don't dwell on it, my friend." The Ranger found a light switch and was pleasantly surprised when the overheads came on. "When we're gone, the people we leave behind, sifting through our mortal trappings will probably be just as disappointed."

Red went to inspect the desk first and Buck went to check the other two sets of stairs. If the Chief Deputy's spatial orientation was correct, the flight leading up -more of a ladder than a set of stairs, would come out in the small shed occupying the corner of the Sheriff's lot, next to the back alley. The stairs leading down, however, ended after about ten steps. A heavy steel door, barred and triple padlocked blocked the way. It was too damn creepy to investigate alone, so Buck rejoined Red at the desk.

"There's not much here at all. Most of it appears to be related to his duties with the county- a pile of arrest reports, inventory, accounting… here are some personal bills, a bank ledger…" Red flipped the cover open, whistling long and low.

The ledger showed a balance of over thirty-two million dollars spread across eight accounts, all of them listed under numbers instead of names. He showed it to Buck, who nearly choked.

"The man was good with money, a right stingy bastard when it came to expenses, but this... this doesn't look right."

As Buck was focused on the ledger and reports, Red took a look at the cork board across from the desk. The photographs were mostly of soldiers in faraway places. In the center of the board was an 8x10 photograph of the Sheriff and three other men. It was the altered version of the photograph they'd found on the Sheriff's body, the one Buck had claimed to have seen numerous times, upstairs on the mantle. Someone had drawn an angry looking stick man where the fifth man should have been and nailed it to the wall with a dagger, right through Ben Hoyle's face. In the trash can beside the desk, Buck found a picture frame, the glass smashed to pieces.

Who brought it down here and why? Red was starting to get an idea.

The newspaper clippings surrounding the picture seemed random: a story out of Mexico about a whole town burned to ground by a mysterious brush fire, a village swallowed by a sink hole in Argentina, a meteor strike in Siberia, a town in Italy leveled by an earthquake, the missing villagers from Roanoke. To Red it made no sense at all.

But the obituaries, however, stood out.

Sprinkled among the news clippings were four of them. Red quickly unpinned them all from the cork board. Each obituary included a set of numbers hidden in the print. Someone, most likely the Sheriff, had meticulously outlined them in red ink. On a hunch, Red compared them to the numbers in the accounting ledger. They all matched one of the eight accounts. Buck couldn't believe what he was seeing.

"I don't believe for a minute that Sheriff Hoyle killed these men and took their money."

Red was surprised that Buck would go right to that assumption.

"I don't doubt that you're right. These men were spread out all over the globe- this one died in Hong Kong, this one in India. That one in Australia..." Red paused for a minute and turned back to the cork board.

Within less than a minute, he'd tacked each of the obituaries next to a news clipping.

"John James died in Hong Kong three weeks ago... his apartment building at the center of a whole city block swallowed by a sink hole. Carl Malone... dead in the Philippines a few days later, the village he lived in completely wiped out by a brush fire, no survivors. Harold Frume, a day later in Italy, an earthquake brought the whole damn mountainside down on his parco. Tommy Dykes, killed in Australia, looks like he was the first, three days before John James- the bridge he was on collapsed under his car. And Frank Unger was allegedly eaten by a tiger in India, just two weeks ago- Sweet Jesus, what a way to go. How did the Sheriff know all these men?"

"That's a rhetorical question, ain't it?" Buck asked, absent-mindedly rubbing his chest. The query went right by Red.

"According to their obituaries, all five of the dead men were war heroes. Army vets who served throughout the European theater and then the Pacific. I would wager that these men all served together with the Sheriff. I'm guessing they found some Nazi gold or something at some point. One dies and their share is split between the others."

Red flipped through the ledger, but beyond the first twenty or so pages, the book was blank. He turned back to the cork board and the clippings.

"The Sheriff did not kill these men, but I do believe someone did. Every one of them died in what looks to be an accident or a natural disaster, but..." Red compared the dates on the obits. All these men died within a two week period, not less than a month ago. All of the deaths looked like accidents, acts of God, but four men that the Sheriff had apparently served with, dying within days of each other, but separated by hundreds, if not thousands of miles?

No way in hell it was coincidence. But how was it pulled off?

"These were not accidents."

"Who would have the resources, the ability to sink a whole goddamned city block? Who would burn out an entire village or bury an entire villa to get to one man?" Buck was getting agitated at what Red might be implying about his former boss.

"I'm pretty sure it's not some insidious plan hatched by the sheriff of a west Texas county, a county that boasts more cattle than people." Ben Hoyle had a good reputation, even if his family had been running the county for over a hundred years.

But then again, there were thirty two million motivating factors to be considered. That much money could tempt even a saint into considering homicide.

"It's only speculation at this point, but I'm guessing someone knows about the millions of dollars these guys were sitting on and wanted a piece of it. I'm guessing it has something to do with the man erased from this photograph."

As Red lingered by the corkboard, Buck began looking in the file cabinet. The folders were filled with nothing more than case reports like the few on the desk. But the deeper he dug through them the more the Chief Deputy realized these files were records of events he had no knowledge of.

"Hey Red, check these out," Buck called the Ranger over to the cabinet. "These reports... none of them have been officially filed." Red took a few of the pages from Buck, flipping through them.

"None of them have a control number from the day book?" Red took another handful of files from Buck and thumbed through them.

"Off the record case files... drunk and disorderly, drunk and disorderly, adultery, adultery, petty theft, embezzlement??? These are black mail files, Buck."

"Ben, Ben, Ben... what in the hell did you have going on?" Buck took the files back from Red, shoving them back in the file cabinet, slamming the drawer shut. Red knew Buck considered the Sheriff as much more than a boss. He'd thought of the man as a son. Red couldn't tell if the old deputy was going to cry or find someone and beat the living daylights out of them.

"Buck, why don't you go upstairs. Get some fresh air. I'll look around here a bit more and then we'll go get some lunch, sort out a plan of action." The Chief Deputy reluctantly agreed with the Ranger. His chest was still fluttery. Maybe some fresh air would help. Besides, he was sure the other deputies were screwing something up, best to go check on them. Maybe that tubby bastard Angstrom had finally showed up...

As soon as Buck was gone, Red began looking at the case files more closely- most of the names were unknown to him, private citizens that had fallen into the Sheriff's crosshairs for whatever reason. Some of the names, however, Red recognized as civic leaders- the mayor of Sego, a councilman from Hoyle, the wife of a county board member, more than half the governing board of the Hoyle County Cattle Ranchers' Association... The sheriff definitely had one hell of a collection in his back pocket, but why?

Red folded up a random selection of the files, tucking them in his pocket. He doubted any of these people would shed some light on the murder, but it wouldn't hurt to rattle a few cages.

He tried the door on the safe, but it was locked. They'd have to get a lock smith in here sooner than later. As to the door at the bottom of the stairs, Red didn't see any keys in the Sheriff's desk. He would check the Sheriff's personal effects when he met with Doc Angstrom regarding the autopsy. Maybe there was something on his key ring that would work.

With nothing more to see in the sheriff's secret vault, Red went back to the cork board, taking down a couple of the photographs- a group shot of a younger Ben Hoyle and about eleven other soldiers, a few landscapes that looked to be somewhere in Asia, probably China, maybe Russia. When he yanked the dagger out of the altered photo of Hoyle and his three buddies, a folded piece of paper slipped from underneath it to the floor. Before it could get soaked in the standing water, Red scooped it up and took it over to the desk. He blotted it dry with his handkerchief, unfolding what looked like an after-action report.

Though heavily redacted, it may have something to do with the man erased from the portrait. Red slipped it into a folder with everything else he'd collected from the vault. He could go over it later, somewhere else. The vault was actually kind of unsettling. Red rolled the file up, shoved it into his back pocket and turned to leave.

But before he set his foot down on the first step, Red froze in place. From the other stairway, the one leading down to the triple locked steel door, he could have sworn he heard something. Red extinguished the lights and crept towards the door, gun in hand.

The underground vault was as silent as a tomb. Red stood at the top of the stairs, against the wall, holding his breath. As soon as he convinced himself that it must have been his ears playing tricks on him- maybe some sort of weird acoustic anomaly from the deputies sifting through the rubble above ground- Red very clearly heard someone let out a sigh on the other side of the steel door and then walk away.

An hour later, Red's fingers still ached from the grip he'd had on his 1911.

Red sat at the end of the lunch counter, ignoring his sandwich, flexing the fingers of his left hand, while pretending to read some of the files he had removed from the Sheriff's vault.

In reality, he was intently listening to the cacophony surrounding him.

Church had let out and the drug store was a hive of activity- women congregated in the few booths by the other end of the counter, trading bits of gossip like boys traded baseball cards; men sat along the counter, randomly spitting out crumbs of information between bites of ham sandwiches and sips of coffee.

By now, the whole county knew Sheriff Ben Hoyle was dead, murdered in a most gruesome manner. They knew that his house was burned to the ground and that his wife's body was found amidst the rubble in a most unnatural state.

Ben Hoyle was well respected, that much was obvious. A war hero born and raised in Hoyle County who, in addition to being the most liked sheriff in county history, was also the director of the church choir, dedicated host of 4H meets and Boy Scout jamborees out at the family ranch, a fair hand with law breakers, and generously charitable towards those in need.

The man was damn near a saint.

Everyone had something to say, but the longer Red listened, the more apparent it became that one woman controlled and dominated the topic of conversation- a blue-haired busy body named Myrtle Griffith.

Her family had been in the county just as long as the Hoyle clan, almost as long as the Hornes. In her mind, that made Myrtle the official recorder of all things relating to the state of affairs in the county. She felt it her duty to protect the reputation of the Sheriff, and she did so with an almost jealous fervor. The more Red listened, the more he came to realize that detail included protecting the Sheriff posthumously from his own wife…

Myrtle didn't think too highly of Marlene Hoyle and most of the women in the drug store openly agreed with her opinion, more than a few of them out of fear, no doubt. No one wanted to be the subject of discussion at the next quilting bee at the Griffith house. To Myrtle Griffith, Marlene was an outsider, just as bad as a carpet-bagger, even though she was born and raised in Call, a small east Texas community just south of Jasper. It was an attitude Red had never understood, and he was from here himself.

The old hens did consider her death a shame, but Marlene only rated the pity through the Grace of God and by way of marriage. Red learned from the all the clucking that Ben had met his bride overseas; she was a nurse with a MASH unit attached to the five hundred and first. After the war ended Ben tracked her down and married her, the Justice of the Peace in Montgomery County officiating.

Marlene had tried hard to fit in, going to church every Sunday, attending the social clubs on Wednesdays, and such, but if your great-great grandparents weren't born in Hoyle County, you were always going to be an outsider. The locals tolerated the military personal moving in because it was the God-fearing American thing to do. And the money the soldiers brought to the local economy provided some much needed stability.

The locals were polite to outsiders, but they didn't mix.

And they damned sure didn't marry.

Red was about to order a fresh cup of coffee when Ms. Griffith worked her way to his end of the counter. Even though his investigation was the talk of the town, no one had seemed to notice the Texas Ranger sitting there alone, drinking coffee, smoking a cigar.

Even with the silver star shining on his chest, Red had a talent for blending in with the crowd, becoming as inconspicuous as a fly on the wall. It was a helpful skill for acquiring candid information. His friends had accused him more than once of being some sort of magician- they often bragged that Red could run across an open field and remain completely invisible if he didn't want to be seen. But when a Miss Myrtle Griffith zeroes in on you, it was like having an atom bomb dropped on your head.

There is not much any man, woman, or child could do in the way of cover.

"You're Andrew Horne, aren't you?"

"Yes, ma'am," Red didn't bother turning to face the woman.

"You're investigating the murder of our dear Sheriff Benjamin Hoyle." It wasn't a statement as much as it was an accusation. Red ignored Myrtle's tone, thanking the counterman for refilling his coffee. He started to raise the cup to his lips when Ms. Griffith curled her lip and continued.

"That seems appropriate, what with your close personal experience with murder. But considering you've been in an asylum for the last two years, I would like to think the authorities would assign someone more... stable."

The entire drug store went silent as everyone turned to watch the blue-haired woman's attempt at dressing down a Texas Ranger.

"Your wife..."

Red pointed a finger at the woman, silencing her instantly. He picked up his coffee cup with his other hand, pausing for a second. After making sure everyone was paying attention, he took a sip. Sitting the cup down, he addressed the silence in the drug store.

"Ma'am, I assure you, I did not spend the last two year in an asylum." Red took a quarter and a dime out of his pocket, laying them on the counter. He gathered up the documents he had been studying and stood to leave. "Where I was and what I have been doing for the last two years is not really any of your business, but what I will tell you is that I did have a lot of time to ponder God's purpose for my life. And the conclusion I came to..." Red paused for a moment, making a quick study of the audience.

He did not relish the attention at all, "Well, that's between me and Him. Right now, my purpose in life is to find out who murdered your good Sheriff and his wife. And then I intend to bring them to justice. Now, if you'll excuse me, Ms. Griffith."

Red tipped his hat to the woman and left the store.

Outside on the sidewalk, the heat was oppressive, but it was nothing like the inside of the drugstore. A thermometer hung under the awning registered one-ten, but as hot as it was, Red was still able to breathe a deep sigh of relief.

He had grown up here, but his two year sabbatical had lowered his tolerances- he just wasn't used to it anymore. Oh, he could deal with the weather- the stifling heat and dry air was easy to endure. It was the people he had a problem with. Their pettiness could just suck the life right out of a man. Right now he would have loved to tell them all to go to hell while retiring to a rocking chair, preferably on a porch with a fan, somewhere in the shade, where the pines were green and a little bit of snow stayed on the ground most of the year.

At thirty-five, a reasonable person would have considered him far too young for a rocking chair. But on more than one occasion, Red had to advise people that the years had nothing to do with it. The many broken bones and the many scars, physical and mental, were all a testament to the many miles Red had put on his lean frame.

Red started across the town square towards the simple, not too ugly brick building that served as the Sheriff's office. The walk twisted and turned under the big, shady ash trees of the park. They at least gave the illusion that it was cooler here than anywhere else, so Red decided to take a seat for moment or three on one of the many wooden benches scattered about. He wasn't expected to meet with Buck until two o'clock- the deputy had opted out of lunch, going by his house for a quick shower and a short nap instead.

Red chose a bench off to the side, away from the crowds of people out and about today. He watched a couple of kids playing tag around the great ancient oak tree standing proudly in the center of the square. A woman was sitting on a bench reading a book while gently rocking her baby in a carriage. A group of men were having a very animated discussion about local politics over on the sidewalk a dozen yards away. And a short, attractive blonde with a baseball bat was running towards him.

Dizzy Cooper came out of nowhere, catching the Ranger completely by surprise. The bat just grazed the crown of Red's Stetson, knocking it from his head as he dove from the bench. But before Red could recover, the slugger swung back around, knocking him hard in the ribs.

They both felt a crack- it could have been bone or maybe the bat. But either way, the girl wasn't satisfied. Dizzy was pulling back for another swing when she was tackled from behind.

For an old man, Buck was surprisingly quick, showing up in the nick of time. Unfortunately for Buck, Dizzy was quicker. She twisted in the chief deputy's arms like a snake, clawing at his face. Her fingers found Buck's right eye, her nailed digging deep into the socket. She ripped the eyeball out before Red could jump in and get the girl in a sleeper hold. She managed to get an elbow in right on his tender ribs, causing stars to blossom across Red's eyes.

The girl broke free from the Ranger, diving for the bat lying in the grass. She rolled over the club, coming up fast. Raising it over her head, she sprinted towards Buck as he crawled along the ground, searching for his missing eye. But she was stopped dead in her tracks by the booming crack of Red's semi-automatic. The bat exploded into a hundred splinters, showering the girl and the chief deputy. She glared at the Ranger kneeling on the ground with a smoking pistol in one hand, clutching his ribs with his other.

Dropping what was left of her weapon, Dizzy Cooper ran like hell. Red let her go despite Buck's insistence that he was alright. Red couldn't breathe without wanting to scream- the pain in his ribs was too intense, over-powering the adrenaline rush of the pursuit. There was no way he was going to catch her.

Holstering his weapon, Red helped Buck to feet. The entire right side of the Chief Deputy's face was covered in blood, his eyeball sitting about five feet away in the grass, staring up through the trees into the cloudless blue sky.

"That's it. I'm retired, right now, this very minute," Buck said as the two men limped towards the street.

The crowd that had come running finally moved in to help. They carried the two men over to the doctor's office, just up the block. Red would swear later, that in the crowd of helping hands was someone who looked a lot like the fifth man in Ben Hoyle's un-doctored photograph.

Red was certain of it.

Red lay on the bed in his motel room, trying not to breath, watching the weather report on the black and white TV. His ribs were bruised, aching like Hell but thankfully, they weren't broken.

He'd declined the pain meds offered by the doc. At the time, he didn't think he'd need them. But now, hours later, Red would have given just about anything for a single ampoule of morphine and the ability to just drift away until tomorrow morning. Instead, he had a bottle of Scotch whiskey and no ice. He could barely stand to drink it neat, but walking around the corner to the ice machine was not something he really felt motivated towards right this minute.

He'd finally gotten comfortable, just drifting off to sleep as the news anchor was signing off, when a brisk, heavy knock fell upon his door. Red tried to get up, but he gave up- the pain in his side was just too much. He slid his hand under the pillow, gripping his .45, hollering that the door was open. When the door swung in, Red jumped out of bed despite the pain.

"Hello George!"

"Andrew Jackson Horne, you little shit!" George Washington Horne strode into the room, grabbing Red in a bear hug.

Red let out a yelp of pain, but his big brother didn't immediately let go. Instead, he squeezed a little harder.

"God *damn*, it's good to see you! You disappear for two years and then out of the blue you call my *office*? What the hell boy?"

"I've been on the job. Watch the ribs, damn it, man!"

George let go of his brother, playfully mussing his hair. Even though Red was a grown man, just ten years younger than George, the older brother still often thought of him as an eight year old boy.

"What the hell happened to you?"

Red gingerly sat on the edge of the bed, holding his side, "Girl trouble."

"You need to date a better class of woman, Jack."

"Don't I know it. And it would probably help if I didn't arrest their brothers for triple homicide."

George chuckled, taking a seat in one of the chairs next to the small table. He opened Red's bottle of Scotch, pouring two fingers in each glass. Leaning forward, he handed one to Red, raising the other. The cheap glasses made a dull clink as the brothers toasted their reunion. George sipped from his glass, but Red slugged the Scotch down as quickly as he could.

"It is good to see you, Jack. But where in the hell have you been for the last two years? After your wife… well, you hauled ass without a word to anyone. We were starting to think you might be dead."

Red grimaced, mostly at the whiskey, but his eyes clouded over at the mention of his wife. He looked down into the empty glass and in spite of

46

the pain in his chest he stood and poured himself another two fingers of Scotch.

"I *was* dead. She… Angela…" Red swallowed his drink. George poured another for Red and himself.

They silently raised their glasses and knocked another round down. After his eyes cleared, Red continued.

"After Angie was gone, I took a leave of absence from the Rangers. I wanted to get as far away from here as I could. Eventually, I wound up in the South Pacific, running a charter fishing boat."

"Sounds like fun."

"You don't know the half of it," Red sat down in the other chair across the table from George. "My boat sank somewhere off the Solomon's and my first mate got eaten by a damn shark. I wound up spending three months on a deserted island with naught but my skivvies and a damp copy of Playboy."

"Which issue?"

"May of '54."

"Ah, yes… Joanne…"

"What did you think of her third nipple?"

"What third nipple?" George asked.

"That's why I'm the detective and you're a pencil pushing lifer in the Air Force. When was the last time you flew anything but a desk?"

Declining to answer that, George smirked and poured another drink, offering to fill his brother's glass. Red waved him off.

"I eventually got picked up by a Navy destroyer group, but they were heading the other way. So I spent a few months with them, chasing down pirates, smugglers, and gun runners. We finally made it to Bangkok where I was able to catch a ride to Tokyo and then on to Frisco. I probably would have been home sooner, but I got hung up in Long Beach, filling out paperwork at the personal support detachment. Would you believe they wanted to charge me for the rescue as well as room and board for the two months I was with the detail?"

"Fucking bureaucrats. The damn bean counters would charge you for the bullets in your gun if they could get away with."

"Well, eventually we came to the mutual understanding that those two months counted towards my time in service. They amended my file and they even cut me a check for a thousand bucks. Sometimes it helps being a goddamn war hero."

"So how long have you been back?"

"In Texas? About three weeks. Got back to Austin on the twentieth of July and they immediately transferred me out to District F, right into a bank robbery case."

The two brothers sat in silence for a minute or two.

Red rolled his empty glass between his hands then got to the point.

"Speaking of war heroes," Red pulled a file folder under the table and slid it across the table towards his brother. "You still have your security clearance?"

George put his glass down on the table with a heavy *thunk*, "I'm the commanding officer of an Air Force bomber group. Of course I do."

"This morning, by complete and total coincidence, I walked into the murder investigation of Sheriff Ben Hoyle. He was found on his sister's front lawn, a three inch hole burned through his head. When we went to notify his wife, we found their home fully engulfed in flames."

George nodded, "I saw the smoke earlier this morning and sent the trucks out from Iron Mesa. Scuttlebutt was that a Ranger was poking around, but I would never have guessed it was you."

Red considered the bottle of Scotch. After a brief second, he filled his empty glass and continued.

"We found a neat little one-shot flamethrower near the backdoor, burnt to a crisp. Near that was the wife's body. She didn't have a scratch on her, other than a perfect three-inch hole through her heart. And, get this… even though the place had completely burned down around her, the body was ice cold. Damn near gave Buck Wyndell a heart attack when we found her. But the kicker was the vault. We found a bunker under the house. Tucked away down there were these…" Red tapped the folder with his finger. George flipped the folder open, the after action report was on top.

"Operation 'black bar'" George chuckled at his own joke. "I've seen more than a few of these." George pulled the heavily redacted file over and thumbed through the few documents.

"This is some heavy duty stuff, brother. This was the kind of operation where if you asked about having the right security clearances you didn't have the right security clearances," George flipped back and forth through the papers, holding them up to the light over the table, a futile attempt to read through the black marker covering almost all of the text.

"These documents are from a debriefing in '46, just before I was assigned to the bomb group out at Iron Mesa- I was still flying at the time. Beyond that, all that I know about this is what was in the newspaper," George tossed the papers down on the table, "eight soldiers showed up in the Port of Houston on a tramp freighter about a year after the war ended. They claimed they had escaped from a Japanese prison camp in mainland China and spent a nearly half a year making their way back home, pure bullshit. It was a covert op into Soviet Russia." George looked through the bottom of his empty glass but sat it back down, picking up the papers again. He inspected the last page for a few seconds, but quickly tossed the documents down again. He got out of his chair, pacing the floor, chewing on his thumb, mulling the information over in his mind. Red allowed his brother to go on like this for a moment or two, but he finally had to speak up.

"I didn't get that from any of those documents. You know more than you're letting on."

George stopped pacing and glared at his little brother.

"Do you still have *your* security clearance?"

Red knew George had taken it the wrong way when he'd asked about it earlier.

"I didn't ask because of the sensitivity of what I had to tell you. I asked because I need information I can't get otherwise. I know you have contacts I can't get to. I need your help, Georgie."

"Ha! My help," George sneered, looking down at his watch. He sat back down across from Red and poured out the last of the scotch between the two glasses.

"What I am about to tell you will more than likely get us both killed," George knocked back his glass and continued.

"You know I was still in the Philippines back in '45. It was the first week of December when this group showed up, fourteen guys in civilian clothes, but it was they were obviously special ops. They were packing cold weather gear and had a crate with them that was never left alone. We were given orders to fly these guys in a stripped down B-29 from Manila to Okinawa, and then over mainland China into Mongolia. At a point near the Russian border, we dropped to twelve hundred feet and shoved these guys out the door. We turned south towards Delhi without even waiting to see if their chutes opened. When we got back to Manila the next day, we were threatened with charges of treason and execution if we even mentioned that we flew that day. I kept my mouth shut and was promoted to flight commander at Iron Mesa. It was almost six months later when the news hit the local papers, about these eight men showing up on a stolen boat. Ben Hoyle was one of them. It made him a local celebrity, as if being born into one of the oldest families in the county wasn't enough." George grabbed Red's glass, finishing the last of whiskey.

"There's a hanger out at Iron Mesa, number eleven. I can't even go in there and I'm the goddamn commanding officer of the whole goddamned installation, a brigadier general for chrissakes. The group that operates out of there, they officially do not exist. This..." George scooped up the report from the table, "this was their operation, before they got some real funding and a license to do whatever the hell it is they do without congressional oversight." George tossed the papers in Red's lap. "Now you know everything I know about it."

"So the odds of getting anything more from this angle are pretty slim?"

George laughed out loud. "You may as well be asking God why we're all here. But, I do know a man who was with the group from the beginning."

"Is he still involved with the day to day operations?"

"No, not at all. He more or less retired about three, maybe four years ago. But from what I understand, they still consult with him from time to time. And he does owe me one hell of a favor."

"Can you set up a meeting? I'd like to ask him a few questions."

"Negative. I'm certain he'd prefer to remain anonymous in all this. If I can, I'll get in touch with him and see if he has any useful information on this."

"When you talk to him, be sure to ask him who this guy is," Red pointed to the fifth man in the photograph. "The rest, I know their names, but this guy," Red pulled the copy of the photograph he'd found in the Sheriff's office, the one where the fifth man had been artfully removed. "Someone went through a lot of trouble to have him removed from this portrait. I'd like to know why."

George compared the two prints to each other.

"Damn, it's like he was never even there."

"Yeah, that is some spectacular work. Not something you could get done at the local drug store."

George pocketed the photographs and stood to go.

"You owe me big for this one. Serious big. The wrong people see me approaching my guy for anything other than a friendly howdy-do..."

"I understand."

"I'm sure you do, but I'm warning you again. If the wrong people hear me asking around about this, it'll be our family portrait missing a few people. I'm not kidding. They will kill me and then, despite that badge of yours," George poked Red in the chest, "they will make you disappear just like the guy in that picture."

53

"That's why I'm only asking for a name. Nothing else."

George headed for the door, pausing with his hand on the knob.

"You know what? You can start paying me back tomorrow. Come by the Double F. Your sister and your nephew moved back from Miskatonic about a year ago. We're having a barbeque."

"What's the occasion?"

"Since when have we ever needed a reason to have a party?"

Monday
August 15, 1955

08:17

Red was up early, but he took his time walking the three blocks over to the Sheriff's office. The ache in his ribs was better, but it could go from dull to sharp and excruciating without warning. It'd be a couple of days before he could get around without a little hitch in his giddy up.

Red still had some loose ends to tidy up on the Cooper case. A wagon was being sent over from Bexar County to pick up Wes and his accomplices; Red's signature was needed on the transfer papers.

When he rounded the last corner, Red was surprised to see Buck sitting on the bench out in front of the office. The Chief Deputy had his feet propped up and a patch over his missing eye. The ever-present filter-less Camel dangled from his crooked smile...

"Morning, Red! I have got something for you..." He jumped to his feet and led Red around to the side of the building.

"You're unusually chipper this morning," Red replied, following Buck through the sally port into the cell block.

"Well, I will be officially retired as of noon today. But there was one loose end I wanted to get out of the way before I rode off into the sunset." Buck showed Red to the first cell on the right.

In the corner, on the floor, trussed up in a straight jacket, was Dizzy Cooper, glowering like a caged animal.

"Damn, Buck, was the jacket really necessary?"

"She damned near tore out my other eye and most of my deputy's hair when we caught up with her last night. We tried handcuffs but she's a goddamn Houdini."

"Well, she can take a ride over to Bexar County with her brother. You hear me, Miss Cooper? In addition to aiding and abetting a fugitive from justice, you're going to be charged with three counts of assaulting a peace officer..."

"Five..." Buck interrupted.

Red mouthed the word back at the chief deputy.

"She beat up two deputies this morning when they tried to bring her breakfast- broke my jailor's arm in two places. I already wrote the report."

"All right then... five counts of assault, aiding and abetting a known fugitive, and theft."

"I didn't steal a goddamn thing, you lying sack of shit!" Dizzy struggled against the jacket, trying to stand up. That's when Red noticed she was actually tied to the toilet.

"You stole my clothes and my best pair of boots yesterday morning. I would have overlooked that, but... you're just not a very nice person."

The girl was still shrieking the most unladylike of curses when Buck and Red walked out of the cell block. Dizzy's brother, three cells down, yelled for her to shut the hell up. Another prisoner started singing an off-key ditty in drunken gibberish. The jailor slammed the heavy steel door shut, silencing the clamor.

Buck sat back down behind his desk and lit another cigarette.

"Never a dull moment, huh? I damned sure won't miss it. No sir, not at all." He pulled open the desk drawer and tossed a set of keys at Red. "Thought you could maybe use these."

They were Red's car keys. He'd almost forgotten about the Mercury parked at the bar down by the river.

"She's out back. I had a county wrecker bring it up early this morning. The battery is fresh and the tank is full. You should be good to go."

Red thanked Buck and slipped the keys in his pocket. He fished out his Zippo and lit a smoke.

"I don't suppose Doc Angstrom's been by?"

Buck pulled a sour face. "That tubby SOB was here earlier, setting the break in Shaw's arm. He said we should drop by the county morgue around eleven to go over the autopsies. You're going to be on your own, though. I'm

heading over to the county commissioners'
court for the swearing in of the new temporary
sheriff at ten o'clock- Moses Reese is taking my
place, a good man. He'll be acting Sheriff until
the election. By eleven o'clock, I plan on being
at least fifty miles on my way to Wyoming."

"So that's it?"

"That's it. I've earned it," Buck took a long
drag on his cigarette and stubbed it out in the
ashtray on his desk. "Forty-plus years, a few
broken bones and one eye ball seems like more
than enough. And after the things I saw
yesterday..." Buck clenched his jaw, "I'll never
forget that," he lit another Camel. "I didn't get
to go to war like you younger fellas. A 4-F
deferment saw to that. I haven't seen half, hell, a
quarter of the things that you have seen. I'm
just an old deputy sheriff in a west Texas cow
town that has more goats than people. I don't
have that callous covering my mind's eye like
you do. So I'm getting the hell out while I still
have one good eye to see with and a few more
years left on the ticker."

Red didn't want to tell the deputy was wrong
about him not being affected by the things
they'd seen yesterday morning. He extended a
hand to Buck and wished him luck. The Chief
Deputy gripped the Ranger's hand like a vise.

"Thanks, Red. And good luck to you, too,
finding the man who killed Ben Hoyle. In spite
of what we found yesterday, he was a good
man. And his wife deserved a hell of a lot better
than she got..." Buck choked up a little. Red

didn't say a word. He gave the deputy a quick nod, pumping his hand once.

Buck took one last look around the office and headed out. He lived the rest of his long days punching a few head of cattle and bouncing his grandkids on his bony knee. Only once did he ever revisit the murder of his boss and friend, Ben Hoyle.

The jailer had the transfer papers spread out on his desk, ready for Red to sign. As he initialed here, here and here, Red asked the man where to find Ben Hoyle's desk.

"Through there," the deputy raised his plastered arm, pointing over Red's shoulder to an open doorway across the bullpen, "But it's only a satellite office. His official office is up in Hoyle."

"That's fine, thank you," Red said. He went in the room and shut the door behind him.

For a satellite office, the room looked well used. The chair behind the desk was almost completely worn out, as was the leather sofa across from the room. A huge map of the county lined one wall from floor to ceiling, covered with push-pins and scraps of note paper. Most were case numbers, a few were personal notes and reminders. Red guessed that it was here that the Sheriff fulfilled his peace officer duties. The office up in Hoyle was probably used for nothing more than ceremony.

The desk was a stark contrast to the one in the vault hidden under the Sheriff's house. Stacks of case files covered the corners. And unlike the files Red had found at the Sheriff's home, these were numbered, logged in the day book, official. A few phone message slips sat in the inbox- nothing out of the ordinary, a call from a councilman (not the one in the secret files) a note from his wife (from Friday, a reminder to pick up eggs) and a message from the Hoyle County Cattle Ranchers' Association (the Sheriff was on their board of Directors, after all) regarding their diamond jubilee in September. Red put these back in the inbox and looked inside the desk.

There was nothing more than pens, pencils and a few rubber bands in the top drawers. The bottom drawer had only a bottle of red eye inside. A few boxes of forty-five long Colt ammunition shared another drawer with the petty cash box.

Nothing jumped out at the Ranger.

He was thumbing through some of the case files when the janitor came in.

Red never even heard the door open.

"You the new sheriff?"

Red looked at the man pushing a trash cart-"Dave" was stitched over his breast pocket.

"No, sir, I'm Captain Jack Horne, Texas Ranger."

"Oh, you're the one looking into Sheriff Ben's killer."

"Yes, sir, that I am," Red said.

"Well, don't mind me. I just came in for the trash." The man pointed to the can under the desk. Red hadn't even noticed it tucked under there.

"Go right ahead. I'm pretty much done here," Red stood to get out of the janitor's way. As the janitor dumped the rubbish into his cart, the flurry of pink phone slips caught Red's eye.

"Hold up a minute," Red reached into the can, pulling out a handful of the messages. He knew he should have looked in the trash can before the janitor came in, but luckily the man hadn't collected anything from the kitchen area at that point. No coffee grounds to dig through.

Red spread the pink slips of paper out on the desk top, sorting them by date and time. With the help of the janitor, the rest of the notes were pulled from the trashcan and laid out with the others.

Starting two weeks ago, the Sheriff began receiving calls from Doctor Edward Cork. One on the second, another call on the fourth; two messages on the fifth, three on the sixth, *five* calls on the seventh...

Between August second and the fourteenth, Ed Cork had called a total of one hundred twenty eight times. The earlier messages were simply tossed in the garbage. The last few days' worth of calls were balled up tightly, some torn in half, the Sheriff's obviously frustrated by the repeated attempts by the physician at conversation.

Ed Cork, Red thought to himself. One of the eight men who made it out of Russia with Ben Hoyle a decade ago; one of the four men in the photograph found on the Sheriff's dead body yesterday morning.

Red picked up the phone and dialed the number on the message.

"Willard Hall Veterans' Hospital, how may I direct your call?"

"Doctor Edward Cork, please."

"Please hold."

Red turned to thank the janitor for helping him sort the messages, but the man was gone. Red never even heard the door open. After five minutes on hold, Red was ready to hang up and go looking for the janitor, but the other end of the line was finally picked back up.

"I'm sorry, sir, there is no Doctor Cork on staff here."

"A patient, then?" Red asked.

"I'm not sure that I'm allowed to share patient information over the phone. Are you family?"

"Well, ma'am, I guess you could say that," Red lied. "Ed and I go way back, serving in the Army together, five years in the same unit. But I haven't seen him in oh, probably eight years. He's left over a hundred messages with my office over the last two weeks, but I was out of town until this morning. I'm just now returning his calls."

Red could hear the receptionist's muffled voice on the other end of the line, a heated discussion with someone else, but he couldn't make out a word they were saying, but the receptionist suddenly came back.

"Doctor Cork is a patient here, but he was transferred to the hospice wing yesterday morning."

"Hospice wing?" That didn't sound good. "Could you transfer my call, please?"

"I'm sorry, sir. The phones in the hospice wing have been unreliable for a few days, but we do have a technician coming out tomorrow. We could give Doctor Cork a message and have him call you back in the morning?"

"You know what? I'm going to be driving over to San Antonio tomorrow. I think I'll just drop by and see him."

"Visitation hours are from ten a.m. to six p.m. Do you know where we are located?"

"Yes, ma'am. Thank you very much."

Red hung up the phone and shoved one of the phone messages in his pocket. The rest he threw back into the janitor's cart as he walked out into the bullpen area. Only the jailor remained in the office, there was no sign of the custodian.

"Where'd the janitor go? I'm done in the office there. He can finish collecting the trash."

The jailor looked at Red as if he had a third eye growing out of the middle of his forehead.

"Huh... I thought Dave was off today," Shaw scratched his head. "I didn't see him come in. Don't see how I could have missed him. I've been sitting here the whole time." The jailer raised his broken arm. "Must be the pain killers. Damn thing hurts like hell."

Red left the jail and went to get some breakfast before heading to the morgue.

The road from Six Guns South to Hoyle
followed the Sego River along the valley floor
like a fraternal twin made of asphalt. For twelve
miles the two snaked together along the verdant
valley floor, crossing over and under each other
like the serpents of a caduceus, finally diverging
from each other for the last eight miles. Over
that final distance, the highway climbed the five
hundred feet up the canyon wall in a fairly
straight shot, the road bed carved and blasted
out of the granite and limestone. The river
below continued to twist and turn until it
reached the Sego Falls, a stepped waterfall
cascading down the canyon wall in six sections,
the tallest about a hundred feet.

The falls made an arc as they descended from
the Willems Plateau to the valley down below,
starting north-to-south at the top, ending east to
west at the base. It was absolutely gorgeous
when the sun was setting, but still beautiful
anytime of the day.

The drive wasn't difficult. Most of the traffic
in and out of Six Guns South was to and from
the Iron Mesa Air Force Base, west of town. But
both the east and north were barely wide enough
for two cars to pass each other. It made for a
nervous ride at times when a big truck loaded
with livestock or textiles rumbled down the
highway, leaving no wiggle room between the

ragged canyon wall and the long drop down to the river.

The Mercury Monterey's flathead V8 chewed up the miles of twisting pavement with ease. Red was able to cut a thirty minute drive down to twenty, arriving at the county coroner's office promptly at eleven.

Red was not, however surprised to find that Doc Angstrom was nowhere to be seen. As the population of Hoyle County grew, the residents had expressed the need for more than one civilian doctor more than a time or two over the past few years, but Red knew it was a sure bet that their complaints had nothing to do with Frank being overworked.

The Ranger parked his car next to the back door, shut off the engine, and kicked back in the driver's seat. Red pulled his hat down low over his face, drifting off for a few minutes while he waited for the doc to show up.

It nearly an hour later when Frank finally pulled up in his Pontiac. By that time, Red had taken a nap, gone through some more of the Sheriff's secret files, walked down to the drug store, had a Coke, a hamburger, and finished a rather nice cigar. Outwardly, Red was cool and fairly relaxed as he watched the doctor fumbling through his keys, trying to unlock the office. Red even hummed a waltz as the fat man led the way to the exam rooms. But inside his head he was buzzing like a swarm of bees. On top of the murder investigation, he was supposed to be out at the old family homestead near Mescalero in fifteen minutes. He was pretty damn sure he'd learn nothing new from the preliminary autopsy report. Patience was not in abundance this morning.

"Buck's not here yet. Do we want to wait for him?" Frank asked, his hand resting on the door to the exam room.

Red hung his hat on a hook in the hallway, shaking his head.

"Buck will be retired in about… an hour ago. And I don't think his replacement will be joining us any time soon. So why don't we just get started?"

Frank agreed, pushing his portly frame through the steel doors. The rush of cool air was nice, but the antiseptic smell nearly knocked Red over.

Two tables occupied the center of the room. On one lay the body of the Sheriff, a crisp white sheet covering him from head to toe. On the other was his wife Marlene. Her sheet was pulled up to her shoulders, her bald head exposed. Red bit down on the inside of his cheek in an attempt to stifle the shock of her appearance.

Marlene's skin had been the familiar bluish white tint of a typical corpse when they found her in the rubble of the burnt-out house. But now it was ice blue and mostly translucent. To Red, it looked almost plastic. Beneath the epidermis, Red could clearly see her veins, fatty tissues, and muscles. Her eyes were still open, staring at the ceiling, crystal clear.

"Red, I have never seen anything like this."

The Ranger reached out to touch the body. Frank slapped Red's hand down like he would a child reaching for a hot stove.

"I wouldn't do that. You ever stick your tongue to a flag pole on a cold winter's day? Your fingers will freeze right to her skin and I'll have to cut you off of her," Frank raised his right hand. Red just now noticed the bandages around the doctor's fingertips.

"What the hell happened to her?"

"Well," Frank took a deep breath. "I have no idea," He sighed. "Whatever it was, it's *still* happening. As time passes, she gets colder and colder. Her body temp was around sixty when I picked her up at the crime scene- hard to say when she actually died, but I'd guess she was killed maybe half an hour before the fire started, around eight. She'd lost forty degrees over three hours. And then this morning, she was close to minus thirty degrees Fahrenheit." Frank pulled on a heavy glove and picked up a thermometer. As he laid the instrument against the corpse, it quickly bottomed out at minus-sixty.

"I don't have any easy way of measuring below that."

Red lifted the sheet from the other body. The Sheriff had been dead not but three hours longer than his wife, but his body was almost completely crystalline.

Red asked Frank if he had any liquid nitrogen on hand.

It was as if a light bulb detonated over the doctor's head. He went to a freezer and pulled out a thermos. "I have some leftover from the junior high field trip last Friday."

Frank sat a paper cup in the hole burned through Marlene's chest and filled it half full of the liquid. Almost instantly, the nitrogen froze solid.

"Wow. They're at least minus three fifty…"

"Obviously you got nowhere with the autopsies," Red said, sliding his hand through the air, careful not to let his bare skin come in contact with the body. Even though he held it two or three inches off the corpse, the cold was almost painful. He flexed his fingers to warm them back up.

"Best I could say is that some sort of foreign mechanism is causing their molecules to stop moving. Completely. They're eventually going to reach absolute zero."

Red had three semesters of physics before he'd quit the college to join the Navy. Thermodynamics was a subject he had spent a great deal of time forgetting, but the concept of entropy wasn't lost to him yet. The closer the temperature came to absolute zero, the rate at which molecules came to a complete rest became much higher.

"I figure the sheriff's already as close to absolute zero as he's going to get, Marlene is not far behind him. Just looking at them, their tissues are almost completely crystalline."

Red took the cup of frozen nitrogen and dropped it on the floor. It broke apart and quickly began to sublimate.

"I'm sorry, Red. I wish I could give you more answers, but I can't do anything with these."

"Don't worry about, Doc. Just sit on 'em for a couple of days while I look into a few other things. I may know someone who knows someone who knows something more about thermodynamics than either of us. Maybe they can tell us why these two appear to be turning into diamonds."

"Diamonds?" Frank perked up a bit as they walked out of the exam room.

"I'm not a scientist by any stretch, but that's what they're starting to look like. If it were me, I'd probably not share this with anyone." Red took his hat from the hook by the door and sat it on his head. "Do *not* let anyone see the bodies, Doc. Like I said, sit on 'em and I'll get back with you in a day or two."

Frank barely acknowledged Red as he left; he was peering through the round windows of the exam room doors in mute wonder.

"Diamonds…"

13:23

Red was an hour and half late when he pulled up in front of the main house at the Double-F Ranch. He was already agitated with himself and Doc Angstrom for being late, the number of cars parked along the driveway just irritated him more. The whole damn clan was here.

Red loved his family, but he had a problem with crowds, regardless of relation.

He stood by his car, weighing his options. The Ranger had never shirked any of the duties set before him in his life, but after two years gone, he wondered if it would just be easier to stay away. He had just about made up his mind to turn tail and head back to his motel room when his niece and nephew seemed to materialize out of nowhere, wrapping themselves around his legs.

"Uncle Jack!" they both shouted, laughing with glee- his brother's daughter and his sister's son.

"Hey, kids! Good Lord, you've gotten big!" Red tried to peel them off, but they only hugged him tighter.

"Where have you been, Uncle Jack?" Jason asked.

"Have you been hunting bad guys?" Jenny asked.

"I've been hunting some very bad men." Red gave up trying to get his legs free. Instead he dragged them along, trying to make it to the front porch.

"Daddy said you were a pirate."

"I told your dad I was *chasing* pirates."

"Mommy said you're a jackass."

"Jason!" Red's sister, Kate, had come out of the house just in time to hear her son.

Red patted Jason on the head, "You're mom's right. I am a jackass."

Kate came down the steps and gave her big brother a hug and a peck on the cheek.

"It's good to see you again."

"It's good to see you, too."

"Kids, let go of your uncle and run around back. You've got a whole platoon of cousins to play with."

Jenny and Jason left their uncle and ran off to play. Red followed Kate into the house.

"Henry out back?"

Kate's stepped faltered slightly, but she kept walking.

"Henry's gone. He left about the same time you did. We had the funeral six weeks ago."

Red stopped Kate with a hand on her elbow.

"I'm sorry."

Kate gave Red's hand a squeeze and smiled. The slap that followed was a surprise.

"That's for running off."

Before Red could stop her, another blow came.

"That's for not being here when mom died."

Red caught her hand before she could slap him a third time.

"Stop it, goddamn it!"

Kate tried to jerk her hand out of Red's grasp, but he wouldn't let go of her wrist. "What

71

was I supposed to do after my wife used my gun to paint the walls of our home with her brains?"

"Your family was..." Kate began to speak, but Red cut her off.

"You ran off to New England and all anybody heard from you was a damn postcard at Christmas. Hell, Jason was two before I even knew I had nephew!"

"At least I sent a card. You breeze back into town and it's three weeks before anyone even knows you're here!"

The two of them squared off, toe to toe, shouting over each other when their older brother, ever the arbitrator, finally stepped into the fray.

"You two better behave." George growled from the kitchen door. He was leaning against the counter, holding a plate of barbeque in his hands. He sat the plate down, licking sauce from his fingers. "Or else I'm going to spank both your behinds, I don't give a damn if you are a couple of grownups. Worse than the kids..."

"Great," Kate muttered under her breath. "Dad's here."

She stomped on Red's boot and pushed past George. The screen door thwacked shut behind her as she stormed out of the house.

"You could have told me about Henry last night, you asshole."

George rolled his eyes as he grabbed a couple of beers from the icebox. He led Red into the den, off the main hallway. Red limped over to a seat in front of the solid oak desk, dropping heavily into the dark leather cushions. George went about closing and locking the doors behind him before handing a bottle of Shiner to Red and taking his own seat behind the desk.

The brothers drank a few swallows in silence.

"I didn't think to tell you about Henry last night. For that I am sorry. Seeing my little brother again for the first time in two years kind of put everything else out of my mind. We've been dealing with yours and Hank's disappearances for so long that we all kind of take it for granted that everyone in the family knows what's going on." After taking another sip of beer, George continued.

"He actually went looking for you."

"What? I hardly knew the guy. We only met at Kate's wedding and then again when you were made Jason's godfather. Why would he come looking for me?"

"He did it for our sister," George absentmindedly peeled the label off his bottle of beer. "You and Kate were thick as thieves growing up, two peas in a pod. And other than Hank, she loved no one more. When Angie killed herself, Kate tried to get down here as fast as she could. But it was the middle of the summer break, she and Henry were on a dig out in the middle of nowhere. By the time they got the message and boarded a train for home, you were gone. It devastated her." George kept picking at the remains of the label on his beer. "Hank couldn't stand to see his wife's heart broken in that way, so he decided to track you down, bring you back home. He left the next morning, flying out to San Francisco, then sailing to New Guinea. He was following rumors of a white devil with a red mustache running guns," George chuckled at that. "You and I both know Henry wasn't much of an adventurer. He was a geologist, for Christ's sake."

"He did alright that one day we took him hunting."

George pshawed at the mental image of his brother-in-law, dressed in flannel with a fur cap on his head.

"He wound up in the Australian outback, God knows how. Three months later, we got one last postcard from Perth and then... nothing."

"I never set foot in Perth, what the hell was he doing there?"

"The post card mentioned some a crazy idea he had about what happened to Rosie."

Red looked hard at George, a cold fire blazing up in his eyes.

"My daughter drowned in Big Hole Lake. That's all there is to it. I'm telling you now, don't bring her up again."

"Fine," George swallowed the last of his beer. The two brothers stared at each other across the old oak desk, not saying anything for a good long minute. George had always been the dominant one, but this time Red did not relent. George finally broke, leaning back his chair, rubbing his eyes.

"Good God, Jack, you're just like the Old Man."

Red took a swallow of beer. "I wouldn't know. Dad never had much time for me. He was a stubborn ass who had to have everything done his way or not at all."

George nodded, agreeing with his little brother. He got up from behind the desk, walking around the room, making sure all the doors were closed and locked, pulling the drapes across the tall windows. Turning on the desk lamp, George motioned for Red to come in closer. He unlocked the drawer in front of him and pulled out a green folder.

He laid it on the desk and after taking a deep breath, he quietly spoke...

"These are some of the files on 'Operation Water Park'," George spun the folder around so Red could read it. He flipped the folder open, fanning the thin, ivory papers out the green leather blotter, the words 'TOP SECRET' stamped in faded red ink across the header of each page. "It's not much more than a roster of the men involved and a list of equipment they took with them. But these men, these twelve soldiers, they were definitely the group I flew into Mongolia back in '45. These other two that went with them, the two that didn't jump but rode with us there and back, they're not named at all. They're listed as numbers. I don't even remember them calling each other by name."

Red picked up the report, glancing through the names- he immediately recognized the three other men in Ben Hoyle's photograph. Three of the other names matched the obituaries he'd found in Ben Hoyle's vault.

George's voice got quieter as he continued.

"Most of the equipment was normal spec-ops inventory for a cold weather forest and mountain recon and rapid assault load out, insulated clothing, skis, climbing gear, small arms and ammunition, light rations. But this one item…" George pointed to a line in the middle of the list. "This is the crate they never left unattended. If any of my aircrew got near it, those two spooks were all over them. The box was about four feet cubed and heavy as Hell. It took four men to lift and carry it. And the place they were going, if they didn't have a truck waiting for them, there was no way they were getting that thing anywhere quick."

"What do you think it was?"

George leaned in closer and mouthed two simple words…

The bomb.

Red drew back, eyes in wide disbelief. His brother sat back in the creaky old chair and crossed his arms over his chest.

"Because of my current job, I am now privy to the various methods of deployment that were under development at the time. What I believe they were carrying was a low yield device that could be broken down into six or seven essential components, re-assembled in the field, and then tactically detonated."

George slid a map over to Red, pointing to a lake on the border of Russia and Mongolia. "This is about where I dropped to 1200 feet and turned south towards India. The best, official information I have says there was never anything there. But the *rumors* I've heard were that Imperial Japan and the Third Reich had a secret facility there, doing all kinds of experiments on POWs... stuff that makes what we heard about in '49 sound like nothing more than some sick kid pulling wings off of flies."

Red remembered those trials- ghastly war crimes perpetrated against American airmen by Unit 731, live vivisections, un-anesthetized surgery, forced infection with deadly disease, and weapons testing. How anything could be more horrific than that, Red couldn't fathom.

"Who is your contact? I want to talk to him personally."

"I can't give you his name."

"Set up a meeting."

"Not going to happen. He knows I'm helping you. He *wants* to help but if the powers that be caught even the slightest hint of a rumor that he's shared this information with us, they would kill him, his family, and anyone who ever knew he even existed. That's after they turn us all into dog food. This group is highly dedicated to their cause," George propped an elbow on the edge of the desk and leveled a finger at Red. "Not a Goddamned thing said in this room was even remotely related to your murder investigation. You and I are here at the family ranch for a welcome home barbeque, nothing more. If anyone asks, we came in here to talk about our brother-in-law and reminisce about The Old Man. Those papers," George pointed to the file in Red's hand, "memorize what you need from them, because before I unlock that door, they're going into the fire- the written report, the folder, the map, all of it."

Red scanned through the names quickly. Of the twelve, he was able to mentally cross off three of the names from the obituaries as well as the four men in the doctored photograph.

That left four names from this list and an extra from the obituaries. Red guessed Frank Unger was one of the two spooks. But why was he with the crew on their boat trip home?

George leaned back in his chair again, his palms flat on the desk, drumming his fingers on the ancient oak.

"Now, it's not my place to tell you how to do your job but if it were me, I would shut this down now. The only thing you're going to find at the end of this row is a dead end."

Red never looked up from the documents.

"There are no dead ends in a murder investigation. Every piece of evidence is a thread. I intend to use each and every thread to braid a rope. And then I will use that rope to hang the killer."

"Just take care that you don't hang yourself and everyone else in the process."

Red handed the papers back to his brother. George took them over to the fireplace and pulled a lighter out of his pocket. The papers quickly went up in flames and one by one, their ashes mixed with those already in the hearth. The map and folder took longer to destroy- Red finished his beer as his brother coaxed the last bit of cardboard to flame. Once all the ashes were indistinguishable from the others, George slapped his little brother on the back.

"Come on, let's get some brisket."

The two brothers came out of the den just in time to see their sister striding towards the front door with a pump action shotgun in her hands.

"What the hell is going on?" George sprinted to get in front of Kate, Red watching from behind. His left hand instinctively went to the butt of his pistol.

"Get the fuck out of my way, Georgie. I am going to kill that old snake."

"Sidewinder?" Red asked.

"Close enough. My ex-father-in-law. That black-hearted bastard *KNOWS* he is not welcome here but he just pulled up the drive in that fucking funeral hearse he likes to ride around in. I aim to kill him before he can set one foot out of that car and onto Horne land. Now get. Out. Of my *way*!" She gave George a shove and kicked the front door open. She racked a round in the chamber as she raised the scatter gun to her shoulder.

"Aleister Corsair, meet your God-forsaken maker!"

Red knocked Kate off her aim just as she squeezed the trigger. The buck shot peppered the front quarter panel of the long black Cadillac. The old man, a bone-thin vulture, grinned like Death despite his daughter-in-law's murderous intent. His driver, a mountain of muscle that more resembled an ape than a man, never even flinched, not in the slightest, when the shotgun boomed. Opening the door for Aleister, he helped the old man out of his seat.

It took all of Red's strength to get the Winchester out of his sister's hands before she could draw another bead on the old man.

"Hullo, Katarina. It is such a pleasure to see you again." The sarcasm was so slight and yet so obvious in his slight accent, a queer blend of New Englander and eastern European.

"You're not welcome here, Aleister." George moved between his sister and the old man.

Aleister's hideous grin never faltered. He looked like an undertaker- black suit, white shirt, black tie, incredibly tall, incredibly gaunt. If you asked someone to describe Death Incarnate, all they would have to do was to point to Aleister Corsair.

"Obviously I am not. Otherwise my beautiful automobile would not have suddenly become so… aerated. Rest assured, I am only briefly stopping by. I have something for my grandson." A wrapped package seemed to materialize in the old man's bony hands. Red heard his nephew shout with glee from a second floor window over the porch. As the boy pounded down the stairs, Kate yelled at her son before he could make it through the front door.

"Jason Henry Horne, you stay inside that goddamn house! If you step one foot on that porch I will *destroy* your bottom!"

The boy slid to a stop at the threshold, torn between receiving his gift and receiving a beating. Red could see the gears running in the boy's head, trying to work out if the beating would be worth the reward.

"You have changed his name," the displeasure in Aleister's eyes was obvious.

"With my Henry dead there is nothing that will ever convince me that Corsair is nothing other than another name for Satan," Kate growled venomously at the old man; Red couldn't understand the hatred his sister had for the old man.

Aleister took two steps forward, placing the box on the grass next to the driveway and then returned to his car. The chauffer moved forward, opening the door for his boss. But before Aleister got in, he turned back to Kate. He started to say something, but thinking better of it, he instead turned to Red and smiled. The Ranger couldn't help the gooseflesh that ran up and down his spine. The old man turned to George, gave a small, almost formal bow and got in the car. As the Caddy rolled down of the driveway, Kate remained stoic, her anger a burning black sun. It wasn't until the car was out of sight that Kate broke down, sobbing almost uncontrollably. Her brothers helped her inside the house and into the den. Her niece brought her a glass of water. Her son kept staring at the package out by the driveway. The crowd in the back yard never realized what had happened in the driveway- the music blared and the rest of the Horne clan laughed and shouted, carrying on with the party.

Later, after the sun had set and much beer and barbeque had been consumed and the guests were starting to head for home, Red pulled George aside, asking just why in the hell their sister tried to kill a man that afternoon.

"Some things are better discussed while the sun is shining and everyone is in a good mood. Forget about it for now. Just be grateful you were able to get that gun out of Kate's hands before you had to arrest her for murder."

In spite of having twenty other things on his mind, Red knew he wouldn't be able to stop wondering about it any time soon.

Tuesday
August 16, 1955

11:37

Red woke up on the couch in his father's den, his head throbbing. His ribs still ached, but they felt much better than yesterday. He didn't open his eyes, but he could feel the sunlight streaming through the tall windows onto his face.

Last night, after everyone else had left, he and his two siblings had opened a bottle of tequila. And then another. And... another?

If Red had to count the number of shots done, it would take all morning to try and remember.

They had talked and laughed about growing up on the Double F. Henry, Aleister, Angie, and Rosie never came up. Neither did Red's two year absence.

Around one in the morning, George and his wife Eloise went home. They lived in the old foreman's house, near Red Hill. Kate had taken over the master suite in the main house when Mother passed away back in May- it was sometime between two and three when she wandered off to bed, leaving Red alone in the old study.

The ranch had been founded in the 1820's. Red's great-great-grandfather, George Franklin Horne, had received a land grant from Mexico when Texas was opened to American settlers. When the Texians began their fight for independence, Frank Horne officially declared his allegiance to the Mexican government, even allowing a garrison to be stationed near Colina Roja. However, the Double F was secretly a major supplier of beef and intelligence to the Texas Army.

Frank Horne made it through the war without a scratch, the Mexican government never knowing he was a spy and (in their eyes) a traitor until long after the fighting had ended. But a few short weeks after Santa Ana was routed at the Battle of San Jacinto, Frank was gunned down by a group of Mexican army deserters, shot in the back while riding home from the stockyards in Hoyle. He left behind a young wife, and an eleven year old son, John Jefferson Horne.

By the time John Horne was thirty-five, he had expanded the ranch up through the deep and wide Blonde River Canyon, across the Willems Plateau all the way to the West Sego River. He was the one who built the main house and established the town of Mescalero.

By the time the War of Northern Aggression broke out, John Horne was 37 and very wealthy. In spite of his views on slavery, he joined the

CSA, taking command of a cavalry unit. Over the course of two years, Captain Horne's lancers were reduced to an infantry unit and eventually absorbed by the regular army. Six months prior to Gettysburg, Union forces overran Horne's unit in Alabama, sending John to a prison camp in Illinois. He should have been sent to the one in Virginia, but the captain refused to leave the men who had been so loyal to him throughout the campaign.

That decision would cost him life.

Captain J. Jefferson Horne was murdered in his sleep, his throat slit by a cousin of the man his second wife had been courting since the day after John left for the war.

As soon as the official news of John's death made it to Hoyle County, Jeanine Monroe Horne and her new beau conspired to auction off as much of the ranch as possible. They were planning on taking the profits and moving to California, but they didn't count on the Captain's son, the child his first wife had died giving birth to, returning from the war. The boy had vanished days after his father rode off to war and was assumed dead. His name was John Andrew Horne.

Being only fifteen when the war broke out, John Andrew was not old enough to serve. But as soon as his father's horse made it over the horizon, John Andrew left the Double F to find a recruiter. He lied about his age, signed up under an assumed name, and went to war. He fought his way all the way through to Gettysburg and then he had to fight all the way home following the surrender of the Confederate Army. It took him three weeks, but he finally rode up the lane to the main house, barely an hour before the auction was to begin. His step-mother's fiancé thought John would be easy to take in a duel.

He thought wrong.

John Andrew Horne put all twelve rounds from his Colt Navy revolvers through the bastard's heart before his body could hit the ground. He told his step-mother to take his half-siblings and be off Horne land before the sun set. Feeling somewhat sorry for the twins (they were only six and innocent in the whole affair) John Andrew gave the woman two thousand dollars, two horses and a wagon.

He never heard from her again.

For the next sixty years, Red's grandfather ran the Double F with an iron will but an even temper, building the herd to over one hundred fifty thousand head of cattle and fathering eleven children. His youngest, Red's father, Benjamin Franklin Horne, had a bad case of wanderlust.

The Old Man joined the Rough Riders at age twenty, and then the Navy the following year. Pop travelled all over the Pacific and deep into the heart of Antarctica, but he never talked about any of his exploits. All that Red ever knew about his dad he had to learn from the old photographs, trinkets and trophies adorning the walls of this study.

The room was more museum than office. It was originally built as a ballroom, seventy five feet wide and one hundred feet deep, with twenty foot ceilings. Artifacts going all the way back to when the first Horne set foot in America filled the hall...

William Frederick Horne's journal, started while crossing the Atlantic in 1622, sat atop a pedestal along with his son's Bible.

John Paul Horne's hunting knives, along with the tomahawk his first son, Jason, had used during the French and Indian War were buried in ancient piece of walnut rescued from the Horne homestead along the Kentucky frontier.

The cutlass carried by Lucas Horne while serving aboard the USS Constitution during the War of 1812 was crossed with John Jefferson Horne's Civil War saber, a placed in high honor above the great fireplace.

George Franklin Horne's dueling pistols sat on the mantel, a gift from Stephen Austin when they crossed over the Sabine River in Texas.

Susie Two Crows Horne's medicine bag and belt, adorned with turquoise and silver, were mounted in a shadow box and hung on the wall. She was Red's great-great grandmother.

The pair of Colt Navy revolvers that Grandpa John Andrew wore during his early days rested in a glass case behind the desk, along with more than a few flintlocks and a blunderbuss or two.

The uniform the Old Man wore when he journeyed through the South Pacific and then to Antarctica was framed on the wall.

More than a few cowboy hats going back nearly a hundred years hung on pegs alongside more than a few helmets and garrison caps.

A dozen or so flags, taken as trophies of war, hung from the walls and a dozen more filled a heavy oak chest.

An apothecary's cabinet containing bits and baubles passed down over eleven generations occupied a corner.

The only time Red had ever been allowed in here while growing up was when the Old Man wanted to "discuss" Red's behavior. It was bad enough being called onto the carpet in front of The Old Man, but to have that much family history staring down at you from the walls while having your ass blistered with not much more than a word or two and angry stare…

In those moments, Red always imagined the ghosts of his ancestors watching with their heads hung low in disappointment. The Horne legacy was a lot to live up to. Even after serving in the Navy for six years and making a name for himself as a Texas Ranger, Red still felt his accomplishments paled in comparison to all the men and women whose lives had filled this room.

Red was still lying on the old leather couch with his eyes closed when he became aware someone was staring at him. He cracked one eye open to find his niece and nephew looking down at him.

"Mom says we can't play until we make sure you're alive."

Red grinned, pulling his arms up to his chest, hooking his fingers into claws, lolling his tongue, and sounding a very convincing death rattle. The kids let out a loud, dejected moan but when Red peeked at them, they pounced, giggling and laughing. He struggled to his feet, throwing Jenny over his shoulder and locking Jason under his arm. He carried them into the kitchen, all three laughing and carrying on. Kate couldn't help nearly choking on her coffee as she laughed out loud.

"I think these belong to you," Red said.

"You can keep them! They're nothing but a couple of pests!"

"Mom!"

"Aunt Kate!"

"Get us down!" They cried as Red spun around in a circle, peals of laughter filling the kitchen. Red let them go, lovingly telling them to get lost. They pretended to pout as they scooted out the door. Red poured himself a cup of coffee and sat down across from his sister.

"They remind me of us as kids."

Kate smiled, sliding the sugar bowl across the table.

"I really am sorry, Kate."

"I'm sorry, too, Jack. We tried to get down here as soon as we heard about Rose and Angela, but Henry's father was so insistent that we finish the excavation that he kept the news from us…"

"It's alright, sis. The past is the past. We learn from it and move on."

"So, now what?"

Red drained his cup and rinsed it out in the sink. He could see Jenny and Jason through the kitchen window, chasing each other around the dooryard with a couple of cap guns. It was hard to tell who was winning, but it didn't really matter. They were having fun.

"Well, I have two murders to solve with very little in the way of leads. It would seem that Ben Hoyle had more than a few secrets and he was definitely a political animal. He might even have been dirty, but I don't think any of that had anything to do with his death. I believe this goes a lot further back," Red paused for a second, sniffing the air. "Speaking of dirty," Red sniffed his armpit and grimaced.

"I need a wash…"

"You know where the shower is. I already put out some fresh towels and found a shirt and a pair of pants that'll fit you."

"Thanks," Red looked at his watch. Good Lord, he thought to himself. It was already noon. "I need to run over to San Antonio before visiting hours are over. One of the two leads I have is a patient over at Willard Hall."

"You know, I volunteer over there once a week. Who are you going to see?"

"A man named Edward Cork. He was a field surgeon back in the war, one of Ben Hoyle's running buddies."

Kate made a face, as if her coffee had gone bitter.

"Hmm, Doctor Cork, I know the guy. He's a jerk. They finally had to put him in a private room. He refuses to sleep with the lights off, really disruptive for the other patients."

"I talked with someone there at the hospital yesterday- she said they moved him to the hospice wing on Monday."

"That's not good. Usually the patients are moved over there when they've got less than a week."

"What's he dying from?"

"Lymphoma. His jacket doesn't say whether or not he was ever exposed to any of the bombs, but I would bet dollars to donuts the cancer is directly related to prolonged exposure to some sort of radiation."

"I don't doubt that at all," Red said, willing away the goose flesh. Cancer was a possible confirmation as to what might have been in the crate the doctor's squad had carried into Russia.

"You've seen his service jacket, do you think you could look up a few others for me?"

Kate drained her cup and reached for a note pad. "I can try..."

Red scribbled down four names and handed the pad back over to Kate. "Be careful poking around into these. And don't mention it to anyone. Not even George."

"Why not George?" Kate ripped the page off the pad, folding it up and tucking it into her jeans pocket.

"Meh, he's worried this won't end well for anyone involved. If he knows I've enlisted your help with this, he'll probably blow a gasket."

"My lips are sealed."

16:00

The trip to San Antonio should have been an easy forty five minute drive, but as it was, Red spent nearly three hours blazing through back roads to get there.

Security police from Iron Mesa Air Force Base had several roadblocks set up on the main highways. Neither his pleasant demeanor nor his badge could get Red any answers as to why. The kid in charge of the first blockade, just east of Coffey, was rude as hell when the Ranger flashed his silver star and asked what was going on. Red had half a mind to strip the airman's M1 Garand out of his hands and shove it up the little bastard's ass as a lesson in good manners. On second thought, that decision would have used up just about every favor Red had left with his brother- not to mention the colossal waste of time it would have been.

Kids these days just don't know what it means to have respect for their elders.

To avoid any other roadblocks, Red had to circle back to the north on pot-holed and rutted ranch roads that were barely more than a pair of game trails cutting across the open range. The Mercury bounced across the field, the suspension creaking and popping in complaint. He landed on a seldom-used county road and headed down into Patch Valley.

While passing through Six Guns South, he stopped long enough to pick up his belongings from the motel. But he didn't give up the room

93

key just yet- he'd paid through the end of the month and he wasn't quite ready to move back into the home he'd abandoned two years ago. In fact, he was planning on putting in for a transfer to another district when this case was done, selling the house in Hoyle- too many bad memories there.

Red made his way up the north valley road and took a quick detour by the county morgue. The doors were locked and there was no sign of Doc Angstrom. He was probably over at his private practice. More than likely, he was out having pie...

Red decided to give him a call later and headed over through Langtry, the last town on the way to San Antone. He saw a few more dark blue jeeps around town, but they weren't running any checkpoints. The Air Force police were parked at one of those drive-in joints, having burgers and fries, slapping the car hop on her ass as she rolled by on her skates- she seemed to enjoy the attention. As he idled past the drive-in, Red thought he saw one of the airmen pointing his way and another reaching for the two-way. Probably just coincidence. The Mercury was kind of flash and Airman Snuffy always liked to play with the radio.

When Red hit the town limits, he pushed the pedal to the floor and the Monterey up to eighty, quickly leaving Langtry and the SPs behind him. Barring any further delays, Red had about a twenty minute drive before hitting San Antonio. He kept one eye out for more roadblocks and the other on the big cumulonimbus clouds rolling in from the northeast. Red didn't recall hearing anything about rain in the weather report, but it would be a welcome relief- it was still pushing one hundred degrees in the shade and the ground was dry and cracked after almost a month with no measurable rainfall.

The clouds kept stacking up, but the rain didn't fall. Flashes of lighting lit the clouds from inside and the swirling winds threatened to spawn a twister. Pulling into the Willard Hall complex, Red checked his watch. It was only four in the afternoon, but it looked more like eight at night. The looming clouds cast a green, gloomy pall over everything.

The VA hospital was the tallest building in the area, built on the only measurable hill on the southwest side of town. A complex of four main buildings, each with three wings ten stories high, was surrounded by three acres of car lots, shady parks, and various support facilities. While he had been in the shower, Kate had made a few calls, finding out where Cork was: top floor, D-building, all the way in the back.

Navigating the narrow roads and the maze of parking lots, Red did his best to follow the sometimes confusing signs that pointed the way. When he finally parked, it was just starting to sprinkle. As he stepped through the big glass doors into the building's lobby, the skies opened up and the rain came pouring down in a blinding torrent.

The coolness inside the building was overwhelming, shocking and almost unnatural. Red shivered, an involuntary chill running from the soles of his feet to the top of his head. His boots echoed on the heavy stone floor as he walked through the reception area. He was slightly irritated that no one was manning the desk.

Leaning against the counter, Red rang the bell and waited for a few minutes, but no one came. He could hear phones ringing, people talking and laughing, but he couldn't figure out where any of the sounds came from. After signing himself into the visitor's log, Red found the elevator, and headed to the tenth floor.

According to Kate, Cork was in room 1019.

The doors slid open and Red stepped out of the car, becoming even more aware of the complete lack of people. Maybe they were having a staff meeting, but Red thought they should at least have someone at the nurse's station; this was a hospital, damn it.

Red's cool demeanor barely concealed nerves that ran throughout his body like taunt, live wires, sizzling with electricity. Something was not right here and Red hated the uneasy feeling, like he was willingly walking into an ambush. Do it once, and if you survived, you will never mistake those cold fingers lightly dancing up and down your spine for anything else.

The corridor of the hospice wing was lined with room after empty room. Inside each should have been the dying- veterans breathing their last breath for God and country. But through every open door, Red saw nothing but unoccupied beds with rumpled sheets. He could hear voices as if they were coming from behind a closed door, but as he made his way down the hall, Red came across no one. By the time he reached the end of the corridor, his shirt was damp with a cold sweat.

And despite his conscious efforts to stop it, he was trembling slightly.

Out of the twenty rooms in this wing, number 1019 was the only one with the door closed. Unaware of the death grip he had on the Colt strapped to his hip, the Ranger gently pushed the door open and stepped over the threshold.

Outside, the clouds grew blacker, lightning flashed longer, and the rain fell harder.

The room was stark white, antiseptic- very clean. The fluorescents overhead allowed for no shadows. The lightning outside the giant plate glass window wasn't enough overpower the electric light bouncing from the blank walls and bare floors. Even the furniture was white. The only source of color in the room was the dead man lying in the bed.

But Ed Cork wasn't quite dead yet.

He stared at the ceiling, laboriously drawing in each breath and holding it, savoring each molecule of oxygen in spite of the obvious pain he was in. Red saw no morphine drip, just a bottle of saline. He couldn't begin to imagine why someone in the end stages of cancer wouldn't want the relief provided by an opiate.

He knew the man was only forty, but he looked ninety.

Red moved towards the bed, but the doctor didn't seem to notice. His eyes were clear and focused, but on what, Red couldn't fathom.

"Doctor Cork…"

The man in the bed didn't seem to acknowledge the Ranger, but Red could see his gaze twitch slightly.

"I'm Captain Jack Horne, Texas Ranger. I'm looking for the man who murdered your friend, Ben Hoyle."

Cork scowled slightly, his lip twitched, and his breathing stopped, long enough to cause Red alarm. When he finally exhaled, Cork spoke in a hoarse whisper.

"Ben Hoyle was a lot of things, but I never called him a friend. So fuck off."

"You left one hundred twenty-eight messages with his office over the last few weeks. As far as I know, he never called you back. I'd love to ask him why, but he's laid out on a cold slab in the morgue, next to his wife, dead, with a perfect three inch hole burned through his face. I found this picture," Red pulled the photograph from his breast pocket and showed it to the doctor. When Cork refused to look at it, Red put it in the doctor's hand. "You, Ben Hoyle, Lucas Brown, Tony Paxton and this man…" Red pointed to the fifth man. "All five of you smiling like you're the best of friends. But for some reason, in every other copy of this photo that I've seen in the Sheriff's possession, this man was erased, completely removed from the picture. Why was that?"

"I don't know. Let me die in peace."

"What's his name, Ed? Was he with you on that mission into Mongolia?"

For the first time, the doctor looked Red in the eye and the Ranger saw stark naked fear, a rabbit cornered by the wolf.

"Who are you?"

"I already told you."

"You're a liar."

Red asked the man "Who do you think I am?"

"I think you're working with *him*," Cork shook the photograph in Red's face. "He can't get inside this room when the lights are on, he can't stand them. They make him sick. He can barely work his magic in here. So he sent you to torture me in my final hours, to drive the guilt home, a rusty nail through my heart. Is this not enough?" the dying man shouted, throwing back the sheets, exposing his naked, cancer-ravaged body. "Is it not enough that I am ringing the bell on the devil's doorstep? Is it not enough that my eternal soul will be scourged for all eternity in the fires of damnation for the things I've done? Now leave me be!"

"Who is this fifth man, Ed?"

"Death!" Cork shrieked, throwing the photo at Red and pulling the sheets back over his frail skin and bones. The man began shivering almost uncontrollably. Red unfolded an extra blanket from the end of the bed, draping it over the dying man. Cork snatched at the fabric, drawing it up to his chin. He stared out the window into the storm with moist eyes.

"What is his name?"

The doctor pulled the blanket tighter to himself, refusing to utter another word.

Red asked again, but got no response. He let out a sigh and turned to go. But as he reached for the door handle, the doctor coughed, muttering under his breath. Red could almost swear the doctor had said 'Lazarus'.

"Beg pardon?" Red asked. The doctor just rolled over on his side, his back to the Ranger.

"I said he doesn't have a name anymore." Red could hear the tears rolling down the doctor's cheek. "Who he was, that man doesn't exist any longer- we killed him. And then *they* turned him into something else. He is no longer Jefferson Lee, he is The Herald."

"The Herald of what?"

"The Herald of Doom, the Harbinger of the Apocalypse."

Red wanted to call bullshit but now he had nailed down a name.

"You killed Jefferson Lee and somehow he has arisen from the grave, looking for revenge." Red walked around the bed and stood between the doctor and the window. Outside, the storm lashed at the glass, but it didn't make a sound.

"You have met him already. He told me that when he came to see me last night. But he can't touch you…"

"When did I meet him, Doc?"

"He watched you while Ben's house burned to the ground, then he tried to stop you from poking around in his office. But you wouldn't have recognized him. He's pretty good at stealing faces from the people he kills, something about residual impressions from the souls he collects."

This gave Red a sick, sinking feeling. He didn't know the janitor at the sheriff's office, but if the doctor was telling the truth…

"If he's been in here then why hasn't he killed *you* yet? There's not a soul in this building but you it would seem."

The doctor laughed, coughing again. This time, it was accompanied by a little bit of blood. Red pulled a tissue from the box on the nightstand, helping the dying man wipe the red spittle from his lips.

"There are people everywhere. All the beds are full, no vacancies in Hell's waiting room. There's been a nurse sitting in that chair by the foot of the bed, reading a fashion magazine the whole time you've been talking." The Ranger looked at the chair, but it was empty. "No, Mister Texas Ranger, he won't kill me. He's thoroughly enjoying the spectacle of the cancer, eating me from within." The doctor's hand shot out from under the blanket, lightning fast, grabbing a handful of Red's shirt. For a dead man, he still had a lot of strength. And he was damned quick.

He pulled Red close and whispered in his ear, "Somehow, you got inside his box."

Red raised an eyebrow as the doctor let go of the Ranger's shirt, cackling with laughter.

"You didn't even notice, did you? You were so cool about it, that's why I assumed you were working with him."

"His box?"

"He's conjured up a box around this room. Hell, for all I know, he's managed to build one around the whole goddamned world by now. Everything outside the box moves and acts just as ordinary as you please. But inside his box, you only see what he wants you to see." Cork coughed again, this time the blood was more than a few drops. "Right now, all that nurse sees is me, sound asleep." Red looked towards the chair again, but he still saw nothing there, neither shadow nor hint that it was occupied. "Looks like all *you* get to see is me. But I'm forced to see everything. You've crossed over to my little slice of purgatory, whether by accident or on purpose, I don't know. Either way, good luck getting back out, Captain Jack Horne, Texas Ranger."

Red stepped back from the dying man as he began laughing again- a thin cackle that became stronger, maniacal, and completely unnerving. Red spun on his heel and walked out the door.

As the Ranger stepped into the hallway, a peal of thunder shook the entire building, causing the lights to flicker and go out. With an audible whoosh and pop, Red was suddenly surrounded by all sorts of people: nurses, orderlies, patients, and visitors, all wandering the halls in the darkness wondering why in the hell the emergency lights weren't on. Red was only momentarily disorientated. The scream from behind the door to room 1019 startled the Ranger back into focus. He spun on his heel, kicking the door open and dashing back inside.

Illuminated by flashes of lightning outside the giant plate glass window, a nurse stood at the end of the doctor's bed, her fists balled up in front of her face, shrieking.

Edward Cork lie bathed in a pool of his own blood. He had used a straight razor, hidden within the folds of his sheets, to slice both his arms open, from wrist to elbow, right down to the bone.

And then, just to be sure, he'd apparently slit his own throat, nearly removing his own head.

Red knew the man was beyond saving the moment he had opened the door. Instead of trying to help the doctor, he grabbed the nurse, turning her away from the slaughter. She buried her head in his chest, sobbing as another doctor and two more nurses rushed into the room.

They made a valiant, but ultimately futile attempt at saving the man, but as they feverishly applied pressure to the doctor's wounds, Edward Cork breathed his last.

As the doctor breathed his last, one last bolt of lightning lit the room, like a flash bulb the size of a light house had gone off. In the afterglow, Red could have sworn he saw another man standing in the corner, smiling with grim satisfaction. But then the lights flickered back to life and no one was there.

Red did his best to comfort the sobbing nurse in his arms. He told her it was alright, that everything would be alright, even though he knew damn well it wasn't.

Red sat in his car, smoking one of his evil black cigars, fuming with frustration as the sun set over the city. He was mentally exhausted and physically drained. As he smoked, he went over the events of the afternoon.

After calming down the nurse, Red had attempted to coordinate a search of the hospital grounds for a slightly Asian or Indian looking man in a black coat, but security didn't want to help. The watch commander assumed the death of Doctor Cork was a suicide, so why bother looking for a suspect? None of the orderlies or nurses had any inclination towards looking around either. Nobody seemed to have cared at all for the dead man.

Ed Cork had had a really bad attitude. Most of the nurses and orderlies thought he was a complete bastard. But some of the staff gave the doctor the benefit of the doubt, rationalizing that it was the cancer chewing him away from the inside out, consuming any decency the man might have once had. They'd seen it before on many occasions.

But Red had a pretty good idea about what was really gnawing at the doctor's soul…

Just what in the hell had happening during that mission back in '45?

The nurse who had been babysitting the now-dead doctor said that Cork had refused any pain medication stronger than an aspirin. He was adamant about having a clear mind right up to the bitter end. And in spite of the pain, the doctor somehow managed to spend most of his time sleeping. When he wasn't asleep, Cork went on horrible rants, laden with every curse word imaginable, questioning the education of the doctors treating him, the dedication of the nurses waiting on him, and the intelligence of the orderlies bathing him and emptying his bed pan.

After three frustratingly fruitless hours of interviews, Red decided to look through the visitor log for anyone who might mourn Cork's passing. He'd had no visitors at all in the two months since he'd been admitted. The Ranger was about to leave on his own when the hospital's director finally showed up, a three star with two MPs in tow.

They physically removed Red from the lobby without hesitation or comment. Outside, three more MPs advised Red to leave the premises immediately, sneering contemptuously at his badge.

It took all of Red's restraint to keep from pounding each of the men into a pulp. They were damned lucky he was done there anyways.

Red drove over to the zone office and tried to get a hold of George on the phone. His sister-in-law, Eloise, picked up on the other end. She told Red that the last she saw of George he was on his way out the door before the sun was even up. Something about facilities inspections on the bombing range. George was miles away from a phone and she didn't know when he'd be back, he often didn't make it home until ten or later- but she'd be more than happy to take a message. Red thanked her, telling her it was no big deal and hung up. He called his sister, but she had no idea why the director would forcibly throw Red out of the hospital. She'd only met the three-star once, in passing. She said he wasn't very involved with the day-to-day operations, that he was more or less a figurehead. Red asked her if she had a chance to get any details regarding the list of names he'd given her that morning, but she had nothing as of yet. One of her girls at the hospital was supposed to call her back tomorrow.

After hanging up with Kate, Red went through the messages in his inbox. Most were nothing, but there was one from Lucas Brown- he had called yesterday morning, wanting a face to face that afternoon. The number he left was to his office, and checking the clock on the wall, it was probably too late for Red to catch him there tonight.

There was also a message from Frank Angstrom, but when he called the morgue, the phone only rang and rang. He tried the doc's home number, but no such luck. Red rang the county hospital, but no one there had seen or heard from Frank since yesterday afternoon, he usually only came in on Wednesdays anyways.

With nothing else to do at the office, Red left, heading nowhere in particular. He spent twenty minutes driving aimlessly around downtown before pulling over into a parking lot outside a grocery store and lighting up a cigar.

After one long last drag, Red tossed the butt out the window and fired up the Mercury. He pealed out of the parking lot, narrowly missing another car as he headed east.

As soon as Red hit the city limits, an overwhelming sense of fatigue set in. Rather than attempting to drive all two hundred miles tonight, he decided to rent a motel room off the highway, just outside of town. No point in falling asleep behind the wheel and becoming a statistic.

The motel was small and clean, right off the main highway. The marquee advertized cold AC and a pool, but no mention of television, which was actually a plus in Red's opinion. Even though the parking lot was just about empty, the only room available was a double on the back side of the property, on the furthest end from the highway. Red didn't complain, at least it would be quiet back there.

Parking his car five doors down from his room, Red pulled his bag from the trunk and slipped inside the room. He was a little concerned that the deadbolt didn't work at all- there was a chain, but that wouldn't deter anyone hell bent on getting in the room. The Ranger jammed a chair under the doorknob, undressed and took a shower.

After standing under a scalding shower for ten minutes, Red slammed hot water tap shut, enduring the bracing cold water until he counted to sixty. He toweled off, inspecting the bruises on his chest in the bathroom mirror. They were still purple brown, but they were already starting to fade. The ribs were still a bit tender, but he had always been a fast healer. He should be at least ninety percent tomorrow. A few deep breaths and twists of the torso confirmed it.

Once clean and dressed, Red walked across the street to a burger joint. The place was all but deserted- a trucker sat at the counter, reading a local paper, the waitress was reading a pulp romance novel, and the cook was playing mop jockey. Red slid into a corner booth, facing the door, and ordered tuna melt on wheat with a glass of tea. When he finished the sandwich, the waitress came back, asking if he wanted desert. He was halfway certain she wasn't just talking pie, but Red declined. She cleared the table and Red wandered back to his room.

Red called the desk for a wakeup call, but no one answered. The room did have an alarm clock, though. Red set it for five thirty. He would be on his way to Houston before the sun rose. He'd ask the ex-sergeant a few questions and then hit him up for lunch. Luke owed him a steak dinner after that business three years ago...

He stripped down to his boxers and lay down on the bed farthest from the door, but his mind just would not slow down.

Red couldn't help but wonder that something went really bad on that mission. Jefferson Lee was left for dead and captured by enemy forces.

Ten years on, he had escaped or was turned loose. Now he was back in the States, exacting revenge on those he blamed for his bad luck. But what kind of weapon leaves a cauterized hole, three inches across and turns the victim into a giant chunk of ice? Was it something that the Japanese and Germans were putting together at the facility? Was that what Hoyle and his crew were sent to destroy?

Also, Red still needed to find Anthony Paxton, the only man unaccounted for in that in that un-doctored photograph. He was dead certain Lee would be making a run at him, too.

Hopefully, Brown could shed more light on the ghost of Jeff Lee than Ed Cork did. In Red's opinion, that man was obviously been bat-shit crazy.

Wednesday

00:05

The rattling door knob jerked Red out of his light sleep.

He instinctively reached for his pistol, but it wasn't where he'd left it under his pillow. He slid from between the sheets and crouched on the floor between the two beds. Except for the soft glow of light coming from around the drapes, the room was as black as pitch. Red quickly felt around in the dark for his gun, his fingers finally brushing over the Colt's checkered maple grips. It had somehow slipped to the floor between the bed and the night stand.

Forty-five in hand, the Ranger crept to the window. Without moving the curtain, he took a look.

Two men stood outside the door. Even though they were now in civilian clothes, Red had no trouble recognizing the MPs from Willard Hall. Why they were here, Red didn't really want to find out, but he knew he didn't have a choice in the matter. One man carried a sawn-off scatter gun, the other held a nightstick and had a pistol tucked in his belt.

Red could hear them talking, but he couldn't quite make out what they were saying. They were clearly agitated that the door had not opened when they tried the knob. Somehow they knew the deadbolt was broken.

Red quietly removed the chair from in front of the door and hugged the narrow strip of wall between the window and the door. The men outside were still discussing what to do when Red gave a yell.

"No room service! I'm trying to sleep in here!"

The two men outside responded by kicking the door in. Red dropped the first one in with a rock hard fist to the temple. The second man, the one with the billy club, stopped short as the lights came up, finding himself staring down the deep dark bore of a nineteen-eleven.

"I'm only asking once, so talk. If you don't answer I'm going to splatter your brains across the parking lot. If I don't like your answers, I'm going to splatter your brains across the parking lot. Who do you work for and why are you here?"

The man on the floor started to get up. Without looking down, Red shot the man through the hand, destroying the shotgun in the process. Red whipped the pistol back up in the second man's face within the blink of an eye.

"Last chance."

"We were sent to scare you off."

"Scare me off of what? The doctor's suicide? Ben Hoyle's murder? Jefferson Lee?"

The man on the floor fumbled with the useless shotgun as he advised his partner to keep his mouth shut. Red shot the man in his other hand, never taking his eyes off the guy in the doorway.

"Who sent you? That three star asshole from the hospital?"

"No, sir," the man replied, never flinching.

"Who then? Speak up or I'll see if I can find the answer by picking through your brains after I blow them out the back of your skull."

"If I tell you, they will kill me."

"What in the hell do you think I'm about to do?"

"I'd rather you kill me than them."

The mewling man on the floor groaned, his mangled hands held close to his chest. Red ignored him.

"You're not really military police, are you? You're with the same outfit that sent Ed Cork and Ben Hoyle and ten other men into Mongolia back in '45."

The man in the doorway seemed to weigh his options. Red could tell by the look in his eyes and the sudden drop in his shoulder the soldier had made his decision. He went for his gun and Red put two rounds through his chest. Before the body dropped, the man on the floor began to writhe and convulse.

"What the..?" Red couldn't believe what was happening. Dropping his gun, he grabbed the man by the jowls, but it was too late- white foam sprayed from the man's lips and then he was dead.

A *suicide* capsule??? Who in the Hell are these guys?

He quickly checked the bodies for identification, keeping an eye out the crowd that was sure to gather. Neither corpse had a wallet nor did anyone come running, in spite the shouting and the repeated thunder cracks of the pistol.

On one man he found a set of car keys and a leather sap. The other had a scrap of paper shoved in his breast pocket with Red's room number written in neat print.

The Ranger dragged the men into the bathroom, dumping them in the tub. Surveying the mess by the room door, Red figured a towel would take care of the blood pool and the deep burgundy carpet would hide the stains. The light spatter on the wood-paneled wall wouldn't be noticed right away. As quickly as he could, Red mopped up the mess, got dressed and packed. After swapping out the half-empty magazine in his pistol, Red left the room, hanging the 'Do Not Disturb' sign on the door.

He quickly made his way through the parking lot to the Mercury, scanning for the soldiers' ride as he walked. There were only three other cars, but the dark blue Chevrolet with absolutely no frills just screamed 'government issue'. Red threw his bag in the trunk of his car before trying the keys on the plain Jane sedan. The Chevy didn't want to turn over right away, but it was the right one. A quick search through the car's glove box and trunk revealed nothing to identify the men or who they worked for. Frustrated but undeterred, he got the car started and pulled it around to his room, backing it up to the door. Five minutes later, both bodies were in the trunk and Red was pulling out onto the highway.

He parked the government car a couple of miles up the road at a deserted garage. He flattened the tires and smashed out the windows, camouflaging it as best he could amongst several other abandoned hulks.

Half an hour later, Red was back in his own car, heading north. He wasn't sure what to do at this point. The investigation went from murder to mayhem in almost no time. He didn't like this situation at all, but Red was as much a realist as he was pragmatist. Two John Doe's affiliated with nameless government agency had kicked in a Texas Ranger's motel room door in the dead of the night. Wasting time trying to explain their bodies to anyone would only slow him down, long enough for their backup to arrive.

He had a place that no one but his brother and sister knew about, up near Enchanted Rock. He could be there well before the sun rose. Hopefully he could catch a couple more hours of sleep before deciding on his next step. He absolutely intended on heading over to Houston, but Red was sure that those two goons had friends that would come looking for 'em when they didn't check in.

The Ranger didn't like giving the impression that he was running from a fight, but he had a feeling that these guys weren't going to back down any time soon. If he could get a hold of

George, convince him to set up a meet with his contact, maybe Red could better plan his next move.

05:30

Red parked the Mercury in the barn about an hour before the sun rose. After driving most of the night he was worn thin, but he wouldn't rest until he was in the cabin, hidden deep in the heart of his twelve-square mile ranch. He pulled a tarp over the car and wheeled his Ariel HT5 out of its stall, into the dooryard. After topping off the tank and strapping his bag to the pillion seat, Red threw a leg over the saddle and kicked the motor over. The 500cc single fired up immediately and Red was off into the pre-dawn darkness.

Red had acquired the land during the war. A good friend, his best friend and commanding officer, Dave Snyder, had no family when he got blown in half by a Japanese landmine in the Philippines. In his will, Snyder left the eight thousand acre hill country ranch to Red.

The property had been sitting idle for decades but as nice as it was, Red didn't have much use for it. The water was good, but the land was too hilly for cattle. He damned sure wasn't going to raise goats or sheep- the Horne clan had been cattlemen for over a hundred years...

About the only thing the Diamond Square Ranch was good for was deer hunting.

Red didn't do much at all with the property for the first two years after returning to the

States. He did some repairs on the ranch house, built another larger barn, and blazed a few trails out to some choice hunting spots, but he didn't spend much time exploring. He was still with the Department of Public Safety at the time. And Angela was still alive...

Red had come out to the property for a few days of down time- it must have been the first week of December, the same year he was recruited by the Rangers. He'd just wrapped up his first case- taking down a particularly vicious group of cattle thieves who had been running roughshod over the Midland-Odessa area. Not only were they stealing livestock, they were running guns into Mexico and heroin back out. Riding with them, deep under cover for nearly four months, Red was a witness to brutalities the likes of which he'd only heard rumors of during the war.

When he'd gathered enough evidence to make the case and time came to make the arrests, Red wound up killing three of the five gang members.

He put the other two in the hospital with his bare hands.

The governor wanted to stick a medal to Red's chest, but before the ink had could dry on the incident report, Red was back at the Diamond Square, mounting his horse, riding out in search of some peace and quiet. He needed some time alone to get himself right before he saw Angie again.

He was deep in the hills and deeper in thought when the storm came- the northeastern was a surprise, eighty mile an hour winds, stinging sleet and snow. Red pointed his horse towards the ranch house, but the whiteout only got worse and they were soon turned around and lost. Red kept his head down, giving the horse free rein to seek shelter.

The mustang found the little box valley on its own- Red would have avoided the creek during a storm at night, but he couldn't see more than five feet in front of his nose. The wind and thunder made it all but impossible to hear the rushing water. In the gathering gloom, the pony sauntered along a trail and up under an overhang of granite. Red wiped the frozen rain from his eyelashes and looked about.

There wasn't much to see out in the darkness beyond the curtain of snow hung from the rocky ledge, but the cut into the cliff-side was deep and dry and completely sheltered from the driving wind. Red found some of dry mesquite logs and with the tinder from his pack, he had a blaze going in no time. As the light of the fire grew stronger, he realized he was actually in the mouth of a cave. He quickly checked for animal sign- there were still some big cats in these parts and a cave like this was a good place to find one. The possibility of a pack of coyotes was on Red's mind as well. He'd heard their lonesome howls on more than a few nights while he and Angela had sat up on the big front porch of the ranch house.

Satisfied that no other critters had been here in a long time, Red stripped down to his bare ass, laying out his wet clothes to dry next to the blazing fire. The bedroll was soaked through as well, so Red lay down in the sand as close to the fire as he could and quickly fell asleep.

Around three in the morning, he woke up, stoked the fire, took a leak, and fell back to sleep. The next morning when Red awoke, blue skies, snow covered hills, and dry clothes were waiting for him. He got dressed, saddled his horse and rode out of the small canyon.

That afternoon, Red came back and set up camp in the mouth of the cave. With a flashlight in one hand and a pistol in the other, he strode deep into the labyrinth.

A system of tunnels and small caverns led the Ranger about a quarter mile back into the hillside. The labyrinth ended in a massive room, three hundred fifty yards across, roughly a hundred feet high, shaped liked a bell, opened to the sky. The floor was mostly even, one side of the room gently sloping towards the north, into a deep pool of crystal clear water. A column of water pouring down through the sixty foot hole the ceiling splashed into the pond, rippling the surface. Rays of sunshine dappled the water, lighting the mossy walls of the cave with a cascade of sparkling light. With clean water and fresh air, Red could set up camp in here and not worry about smoking himself to death.

Several smaller chambers opened off the main room. A couple of them contained the remains of human habitation- tumbled down walls of stone, petrified timber, a few broken pieces of pottery. So it was not a surprise then, for Red to find the cave paintings. Beautiful renderings of deer and antelope interspersed with human figures- hunters stalking their prey as well as gatherers in a field of corn. There was also a painting of a mesa. To Red, it looked a lot like the one on the north end of the Double F-the Iron Mesa, the spiritual nexus of the region for millennia.

People had been in this area for well over ten thousand years, some of them Red's ancestors. His great-great-grandmother, Susie Two Crows, was the only daughter of a Mescalero medicine man. Legend said he was five hundred years old, but as Red got older, he grew to believe his cousins he had spent much of his youth growing up with had been pulling his leg. They told many tales while they went about scouring the countryside, exploring the west Texas wilderness, hunting arrowheads and small game. They'd found many caves and many pictograms on their walls, but some of the paintings in Red's caverns were like nothing he had ever seen. They were absolutely gorgeous, the most artistically modern and realistic he'd ever laid eyes on. In his opinion, they were only a generation away from rivaling the Old Masters. And these were done with charcoal and vegetable ink on a rock wall.

They were a joy to look at, which made Red's private getaway all the more special and dear.

From 1949 to 1953, Red and his wife worked on securing and improving the site. First and foremost, they built a stone wall with a heavy wooden door at the mouth of the cave, down by the creek. They had a small, temporary corral for their horses under the overhang, but seeing as how it could be months between visits to the ranch, they needed a more practical solution, one that didn't require having someone up here when he or Angie couldn't be around to take care of the animal. So he traded their pair of mustangs for an off-road motorcycle and a surplus Army jeep. Angie had been very sad to see the ponies go, but the trade had actually been her idea.

The second improvement they had made was inside the giant main cavern. They built a cabin, a simple two room wooden structure with a long tin chimney that running up the rock wall to the hole in the ceiling. Often, Red daydreamed about rebuilding the ancient stone structures left in ruins when the former occupants left the area.

Red constructed a pier out over the water; the pool was directly linked to the creek and had plenty of bass and perch swimming around in it. Red often enjoyed sitting on the pier, fishing at noontime. Angie loved to swim in the pool at night when the full moon was directly overhead, shining down through the ceiling.

Red loved to watch her.

Whenever he visited the ranch without Angela, Red would lock up his car in the barn by the main house, taking the motorcycle out into the hills along narrow game trails. They wound through the mesquite, sage and oak in a maze that anyone else would easily get lost in. But Red knew every square foot of the twelve and a half square mile property like the back of his hand. He never took the same trail to the cave twice in a row.

During the last year that they were together, Red sometimes worried out loud to Angie that he was becoming one paranoid son of a bitch. But she would belay his concerns, rationalizing his behavior for him in any number of ways...

Over the course of his career, Red had made more than a few high-profile enemies. They in turn, had any number of allies and underlings who'd like nothing better than to catch the Ranger alone in the back country, making a name for themselves by taking out Captain Jack Horne.

Mostly, Red just cherished his privacy. When he was not working, he just didn't really care to be around people at all. He was perfectly happy with just his Angie and some peace and quiet out in the hills.

His brother and sister had been out to the ranch more than a few times for a barbeque or two over the years, but Red had never brought them out to the caves. So when he rounded the last bend in the trail, he was a bit taken by surprise seeing a jeep parked under the overhang by the entrance to the cave.

Finding his brother George leaning against the wall next to the heavy wooden doors of his sanctum sanctorum, smoking a cigarette, just as easy as you please was infuriating to say the least.

Red parked the Ariel, primed to explode. But as he got closer, he could see George's face. His brother had one eye black and a broken nose.

"What the hell happened to you?"

George stepped off the wall, flicking his cigarette into the sand.

"Couple of no name goons came by the office, wondering what you knew about Ben Hoyle's time in the military. They weren't too happy with my answers."

Red's anger was instantly redirected.

"When?"

"About an hour after lunch, yesterday. They caught me out on the bomb range, doing some shelter inspections. They put my assistant in the hospital and I thought they were going to kill me. But they were in a hurry. They already knew you were on your way to San Antonio."

Red walked over to the creek, plunging his hand in the clear cold water. He yanked on a slender chain, pulling a heavy brass key out from under a rock. He strode past his brother and unlocked the doors to the caves. "Were these two clowns about five eight with matching crew cuts?"

"Yeah," George replied.

"One was blonde with a dimple in his chin and the other missing a chunk of his left ear?"

"Yep, that's them."

Red told his brother to wheel the bike through the heavy doors as he got in the jeep.

He started the Willys up and pulled it up behind the Ariel. Red jumped down and pulled the heavy doors shut.

"Well," Red slid a wrist-thick forged steel bolt home, "they aren't anyone's problem now."

Red made a slashing motion across his throat with his thumb as he stepped past his brother into the stone hallway. He pretended not to notice George's forced concern.

"They catch you at the VA hospital? Wow..." George's line of questioning was interrupted when they stepped out into the massive main cavern. He was awed by the size of the cave and the water falling through the ceiling into the crystal pond. Red had to turn around and grab his brother's sleeve, dragging him along to the cabin.

"There were too many people around for them to try anything at the hospital. They tried to get the jump on me later, at that little no-tell motel just west of Seguin. I left their bodies in the trunk of their car. They were in Army uniforms- military police- when I first saw them, but neither had any identification. I couldn't get the one to tell me who they were working for. The other ate a suicide pill." Red stopped on the cabin's steps and turned to his brother.

"How in the hell did you find this place?"

"When you disappeared two years ago, your sister and I were worried you might have done something stupid. I came up here more than once looking for you, following your trails through the back country. You weren't the only one grandpa taught to read trail sign, but you sure as hell didn't make it easy. I never could get in here, though... This place is amazing. A man could die happy in here."

"Hopefully you didn't make it too easy for anyone to follow you this morning," Red glowered. He went into the cabin and lit the lantern over the table. George stood in the doorway, still admiring the cave and its pond.

"You are waiting for an engraved invitation? Come on in."

George stepped inside, shutting the door behind him.

Red was already out of his boots and reclining on his bunk. "There's only the one bed, but I do have a sleeping bag over there in the corner. You're welcome to use it and the couch."

"I'm not tired."

Red rolled over, his back towards his brother. "Well, I am exhausted. Killing two men and then driving all night tends to take a bit out of a body."

"They're Sector Eleven."

Red cocked his head towards his brother for a brief moment and then turned back to the wall, settling into the feather mattress.

"Yeah, I kind of figured as much. There's a Thompson in the footlocker, under the table, and there's a shotgun over the door if that ain't enough. Get a few hours of shut eye and then we'll figure out something over lunch."

George wasn't used to taking orders from his little brother. He stood in the middle of the room, undecided about what to do.

Before he could unroll the sleeping bag, Red was sound asleep, lightly snoring.

If a former Navy commando turned Texas Ranger thought it was safe enough to get some sleep, George figured it was a pretty good time to get some sleep. He rolled the bag out on the couch and kicked his shoes off.

He was unconscious as soon as his head hit the pillow.

After three hours of sleep, Red was up and moving. He quietly got dressed while his brother snored deep inside the sleeping bag on the ancient leather couch. He skipped the coffee, knowing that it would wake George, and Red wasn't quite ready to talk to him yet. He left the cavern hideaway, taking his brother's jeep over to the main ranch house.

Looking through the screen of trees towards the main house, Red could see faint whispers of smoke rising into the clear blue sky. He parked the jeep, striking out on foot, creeping through the last half mile of brush. As he got closer to the house, Red could hear several voices and the crackle and pop of a dying fire. He slowed his pace, crawling along on his belly under thick bushes and around the few cacti.

At the edge of the yard, he parted the tall grass and peered out at the destruction.

Red's blood boiled when he saw the house was a smoking ruin.

Three men armed with sub-machine guns were leaning up against the hood of a navy blue sedan, another Government Issue car. At their feet were several flamethrowers of the same design as the throw-away device Red had found in Ben Hoyle's ruined house. From his vantage point in the grass, Red could see a fourth man sitting in the second floor window of the barn with a rifle, smoking a cigarette and hollering bad jokes down to his companions.

They had no idea they were being watched.

As he listened to the idle talk between the jokes and bouts of laughter, Red gathered that a little bird had told them about the hill country hideaway. One of the men was wondering if the little bird might know where the Ranger could be hiding out in the hills. The second man told him that their orders were to wait for the bird to show up before doing anything else. The third man, however, just about had the other three ready disobey those orders. He was anxious to find the Ranger, working hard to convincing them on heading out and searching of the property. They needed to wait for the fire to die down, the first man said. They didn't want to scorch the whole countryside while they were out in it. The second man tapped one of the flamethrowers with his boot, saying they'd light that fire after they killed the Ranger and were heading back to town.

As the fools kept chit-chatting with each other and laughing at the random one-liners thrown down by the sniper in the loft, Red made his way around to the back side of the barn and silently slipped inside.

From a scabbard screwed to the underside of the tool bench, he drew a ten inch bayonet. He crept to the ladder leading to the loft, skirting the Mercury, his anger a simmering pool of black bile. The tarp had been ripped away and the hood was up, engine wrecked- plugs wires cut, hoses slit from radiator to engine block, and battery cables ripped away. The G-men didn't want him leaving if he came through here while they were traipsing through the brush.

Clenching the blade between his teeth, he climbed the ladder, making sure to avoid the third and eighth rungs- they had squeaked and squealed like the gates of Hell.

Once on the platform, Red hugged the wall, keeping to the sniper's back. He slipped up behind the man completely undetected. The man was oblivious, his situational awareness was non-existent. With his rifle leaning against the wall, one leg dangling out the window, fiddling around with his cigarette lighter, telling one bad joke after another, the sniper was a too easy target.

Red waited for the last punch line and the braying response from the yard. As the men below were bent over laughing, Red grabbed a handful of the comedian's hair and yanked his head back. The razor sharp blade sliced through the windpipe before the man could cry out.

Red carefully pulled the body back into the window, never taking an eye off the men below. They were too busy repeating the punch line and chuckling amongst themselves, to notice their jester was dead. Red found that he recognized two of the men. They were the pair of military men that had been standing apart from the crowds watching the Sheriff's house burn to the ground Sunday morning. They had managed to vanish under cover of smoke that morning, but today, there was no escaping the Ranger.

He picked up the rifle and chose his first target. Red had noticed it before making his way into the barn- the idiots had left the pressure valve on their spare flamethrowers open.

Who builds a flame thrower with a lever actuated ball valve?

Dead men do.

One steady pull through the trigger and the flamethrower exploded in a shower of napalm. Two of the men and the hood of their car were doused from head to toe with ropes of jellied gasoline. Red flipped open the dead sniper's lighter, spinning the wheel. He calmly tossed it out the window, curling his lip as the entire dooryard erupted in a cloud of brilliant orange flame and oily black smoke. The two men tried to drop and roll, but the ground was a lake of fire, burning bright across the thirty square feet of dried grass. The third man on the ground had escaped the inferno unscathed and was sprinting up the drive, hoping for an escape via the highway.

In Red's lifetime, he had dropped too many a white tail deer at a dead run to miss. He took aim through the rifle's scope and slowed his breathing, listening to his heart rate. Between beats ten and eleven, Red squeezed the trigger.

The round of thirty-aught-six exploded the man's right knee, sending him down in a shrieking sniveling bleeding heap. His lower leg was left barely connected by a tenuous thread of tendon, artery, and vein.

Red slung the rifle over his shoulder and calmly climbed down out of the loft. The screams of the burning men had ceased by this point, their bodies curled into fetal balls of burning flesh. The corpses sizzled and popped as Red leaned down, lighting a cigar with their flame.

The last man was still in the road, one hand clutching the rosary he had been wearing around his neck, his other hand clawing at the dirt, dragging himself towards his submachine gun.

Red crouched down over the weapon and held the bleeding man's gaze with an unflinching eye. The rage behind Red's stare was as black as the cigar clamped between his teeth.

He looked over the man's mangled leg, tut-tutted, shaking his head.

"Now that looks like it hurts."

The man broke Red's stare and glanced down at his knee. His whole body started trembling and shaking. Shock was overcoming the adrenaline dump.

It wouldn't be long now.

Red searched the sky for the sun, but it was still hiding behind the row of trees up on the ridge line. He held up his hand, and with his fingers, estimated it would be less than half an hour before the entire valley was baking under clear blue skies. The man on the ground didn't know or didn't seem to care, continuing his crawl towards the machine gun.

Each time his fingers were just about to close on the stock, Red would slide the gun a few more inches from the man's grasp. Red must have done this three, maybe four times and yet, the man continued to struggle towards the weapon.

"You really want that, don't you? What in the world did I do to rate such intense determination?"

The man on the ground didn't answer. He kept clawing at the dirt, inching towards the gun.

"This is going to get old pretty damn quick, son."

"I'll never talk."

"Well now, I didn't expect that you would. But, just so you know, neither did those two buddies of yours, the ones that came knocking on my motel room door last night? Do you want to know where they are now?" Red examined the cherry on his cigar, taking a few puffs and offering to share with the man crawling in the dirt. The soldier declined, continuing to struggle towards the weapon. "Their carcasses are broiling in the trunk of their car." Red slid the gun a few more inches away from the man's reaching hand. "No, I wholly expect that you will take whatever secrets you have with you to your grave, which, when all things are considered, will most likely be that patch of road right there."

The man, a kid really, probably not older than twenty-three, stopped dragging himself through the dirt and put his face down. His breathing was becoming shallow, his skin turning grey.

"You're going to die here, son. And I will leave your corpse right there to bloat in the sun. Your belly will expand until it explodes and then the coyotes and buzzards will fight over your rotting meat as flies lay their eggs in your eye sockets. The maggots will crawl through your entrails and eventually, after all the flesh has been stripped away, your bones will be scattered and bleached by the sun. Centuries from now, when the world is one giant city from shore to shore, someone may come along, digging up the ground to set the foundations of some new skyscraper and they might pull your skull out of the dirt. They'll wonder for a minute or two about who you were, why you died here, but ultimately, they will toss your bones aside and move on."

"I am not afraid to die for my country."

Red's gaze became more intense- blacker, deadlier.

"And I am not afraid to kill for that same country. I have. More times than you can probably count. You are just another meat bag in a long line of assholes that have gotten in my way."

The man broke, sobbing once. And then was still. For a second, Red thought he had passed on. But then the man spoke quietly through the dirt.

"I don't know anything. They don't tell us the why of the missions, only that they must be done."

"So tell me, how does it feel?"

"How does what feel?"

Red lifted the man's head up and looked him in the eyes.

"How does it feel to be nothing more than a tool, something to be used up and discarded? Your superiors don't give a damn about you. You have but two purposes so far as they're concerned. Pull a trigger and or take a bullet." Red softened his tone a bit, "Now, I know how it feels. I've been there." He reached down, fingering the cross around the man's neck. "But my eyes were finally opened before I had to find myself standing before the Throne, making a full account of myself and my time on this earth before God Almighty. Do you want to meet your Maker with that written in the book that is your soul? That you willingly allowed yourself to be subjugated and used for something far below what God intended?"

The man closed his eyes and put his head down again.

"I'll never talk."

Red stood up with the man's machine gun in his hand. He pulled the magazine out and checked the action. He emptied the weapon of all but one round, pocketing the extra ammunition and then reinserting the magazine. He walked about four feet in front of the man and placed the gun in the dirt.

"You've got one bullet, make the most of it."

Camp Carter was easily an hour south of the ranch, but Red made it in forty minutes.

He pushed the Willys well beyond its limits, very nearly rolling it over more than twice. The jeep's little four cylinder complained up every hill, the clutch shuddered through every shift. Red wasn't sure the vehicle would ever run right again after this, but he would not relent until he reach the town limits.

When he hit the main drag, Red slowed his pace but maintained a direct route- the only pay phone in town was in the diner and he didn't really care who saw him using it. In fact, he was hoping for an audience.

When he pulled up in front of Cactus Jack's diner, he immediately took notice of the two men in a black Dodge parked across the street. They were trying to maintain a low profile, but in a small town like this, they stuck out like a sore thumb, obvious G-men. Red tipped his hat in their direction as he stepped inside the crowded restaurant.

"Hey, Ranger Red! How're you doing?" Cactus Jack greeted Red from behind the counter. He was a small man, pushing seventy, but he had the constitution of a forty year old. Red had known him since childhood.

"Jack, I'm in a bit of a hurry. I'll fill you in after I get off the phone."

"Important business, I'm sure. I'll grill you up a steak and some eggs."

136

"You might want to hold off on that a minute," Red said, stepping into the phone booth by the back door. Dropping a dime in the slot, he dialed the main house at the Double F. As he talked to the foreman- his closest cousin, Fred Mueller, the two men from the Dodge walked in and sat down at the counter. They ignored Cactus Jack and were rude as hell with the waitress. They glared at Red, waiting for him finish.

Red turned his back to them and asked Fred to put his sister on the phone.

"Any word on those four names I gave you yesterday?"

"All four service jackets were sealed Monday afternoon. You're not going to like it when you find out whose name is on the order..."

"I already have a pretty good idea who it is."

After talking to Kate for a half minute longer, Red disconnected and made another call.

The two men at the counter didn't notice the phone ringing in the kitchen.

That call only took seconds, but Red held the phone to his ear and made a show of chatting up somebody, turning and waving at the two goons. The one on the right started to get up, but one on the left grabbed him by his sleeve, yanking his partner back down onto the barstool. After sixty seconds had passed, Red hung up the phone and stepped out of the booth, making for the back door. The two men at the counter jumped up from their seats, advancing towards Red. Cactus Jack pulled a shotgun up from under the

137

counter, stepping between the men and the back door.

The massive bore of the sawn-off twelve gauge slowed them down, allowing Red enough time to duck out the back and get in Jack's bright blue Ford F-1.

Francene was parked right where Cactus Jack said she would be, the keys in the ignition. The engine roared to life without hesitation and Red threw the truck into gear, stomping on the gas. As Francene caught traction and peeled around the corner, Red caught a glimpse of the two men running out the back door of the diner. One threw his hat down as the other ran around to the front of the restaurant to get their car.

It took nearly a mile for them to catch up, but only because Red was taking his time. In another life, Cactus Jack had been a moonshiner with a reputation for building mills that outperformed everything on the road, especially T-men and G-men. Francene could have very easily dusted the government-issue Dodge, but Red didn't want to completely lose them.

He wanted them to follow.

He made like he was heading back towards the Diamond Square, but instead of the more direct route to the north east, he took the northwestern highway. The Dodge struggled to keep up on the few straight aways, but they were able to close the gap on the curves. As powerful as the Ford truck was, Francene just wasn't made for high speed maneuvering. But

Cactus Jack had taught Red how to drive when he was only twelve. Red down shifted into the turns and punched it out the other side. The rumble and roar from the dual exhaust sounded like a pride of lions chasing the devil.

The back gate to the Diamond Square was about twenty miles away but before Red would reach that sanctuary, the road crossed over the upper Sego River Canyon- one of the highest highway bridges in the southwest.

Three miles from the bridge, Red slammed the truck into second and dumped the clutch, the gear box protesting loudly, instantly dropping the speed to forty. Closing the gap, the Dodge's bumper kissed the Ford's rear end before backing off by only a few feet. In his rearview mirror, Red watched the passenger reaching out the window with a handgun. Red mashed the brakes and dropped the truck into first- the Dodge slammed into the Ford, locking bumpers. The gunman was thrown forward, dropping the revolver on the road. The driver smacked the steering wheel with his face.

Grinning like a skull stripped of all its flesh Red watched the driver spit broken teeth out his window. Satisfied, the Ranger put his foot through the floor, the rear tires breaking loose as the V8 raged, a wild beast trapped under the hood. Shifting to second, the truck launched itself from the Dodge like a rocket, ripping away its front bumper. Red never let up, foot to the floor, pushing the Ford over sixty before shifting into third. He found fourth and wound the mill up over one twenty, leaving the Dodge behind in a cloud of exhaust and road dust.

But the driver of the sedan didn't give up easily. With the sleeve of his crisp white shirt, he wiped the blood from his nose and lacerated lip. He kept the throttle wide open, pedal to the floor. He pulled the revolver from his shoulder holster, handing it to his partner...

"Kill him."

"Our orders are to bring him in alive!"

The driver cuffed the passenger with the .38, "Screw orders! Take the damn gun and when we catch up to him, put a bullet right between his squinty blue eyes!"

The Dodge roared around the last bend before the Sego Canyon Bridge to find their prize parked across both lanes of the highway.

The Texas Ranger was waiting.

The driver jerked the wheel over to the left, jamming on the brakes, yelling for his partner to fire! Fire! *FIRE!!!* But before the other man could draw a bead, Red put two slugs from his forty-five through the right front tire of the Dodge. The driver lost control of the sedan, its front end digging into the asphalt. The car pitched over, rolling seven times, barely missing Francene by a fraction of an inch as it crashed through the guard rail, sailing into empty space.

Red could hear the men screaming as the Dodge plummeted the two hundred and ninety feet to the rushing river below.

Grimly satisfied, Red put the Ford in gear, spinning the truck around, heading for the Diamond Square. Before he got off the bridge, he stopped the truck and yanked the Dodge's bumper from Francene's, tossing it over the side into the river. He climbed in the cab and headed for the ranch.

Over the past twelve hours, Red put eight men in their graves- he would like to know why. He also wanted the name of George's contact with Section Eleven, but he already had a pretty damned good idea who that was.

As the bodies stacked up like cord wood, finding who murdered Sheriff Hoyle was fast becoming secondary to finding out why someone wanted Red off the trail.

George looked at his watch as soon as he opened his eyes. He'd been asleep for about seven hours.

Sitting up, George looked towards the bunk, but his little brother wasn't there. George threw back the covers, swinging his feet onto the smooth wooden floor. He ran a hand across his buzz cut and yawned deep enough to make his jaw pop. His face was tender from yesterday, but the swelling had gone down quite a bit. The man who threw the punch knew what he was doing.

He was about to get up and put on a pot of coffee when he heard the metallic snap of a lighter being closed.

"Mornin', big brother."

George nearly jumped out of his skin when Red spoke. The Ranger had been sitting at the table playing solitaire, not twenty feet away, completely unnoticed.

"Hellfire and damnation, Jack. You just about gave me a heart attack."

Red tapped his fingers on the table top, inches away from his forty-five, never taking his gaze off his brother.

"What's going on?" George tried to play down his jumpiness, but his brother had unnerved him.

"I went down to the house this morning, to make a few calls, but I couldn't use that phone.

So I had to ride into town and use the one at Cactus Jack's place."

"You should've gotten me up, I'd have ridden in with… wait, why couldn't you use the phone in the house?"

Red flipped a card over on the table, the three of diamonds.

"The place had been burned to the ground."

"What? How?"

"Arson," Red flipped over another card, six of clubs.

George fell back into the couch, looking up at the ceiling. "I told you this was going to get bad."

"You don't know the half of it, big brother."

George looked Red in the eye, but only for an instant. He could no longer match his little brother's gaze, even for a second.

"There were four of them. Three went down hard, but the fourth… well, Georgie, he sang like a canary."

George closed his eyes and whispered, "Impossible."

"How's that, George? Conditioning? Training? A suicide capsule between the cheek and gum?" Red watched George closely, his fingers still tapping a soft staccato beat on the table top. "Our song bird was a greenhorn, out on his first assignment from what I gathered. I'm guessing he was recruited right out of the academy. The fool forgot his black capsule in his shirt pocket. After I burned off both his feet and his left hand, he told me all kinds of interesting things. Like why Section Eleven is

143

trying to stop my investigation. Like… who his commanding officer is."

George deflated like a balloon. His right hand slid from under a pillow but before he could level the thirty-eight, Red put a single round through his brother's chest. The revolver clattered to the floor and George looked down at his shirt, a blossom of red spreading across his chest. He tried to draw a deep breath but the bullet had pierced a lung.

"I'm sorry, Jack…"

"I know you're sorry, goddamn you George. It didn't have to be like this."

"This… is bigger… than us… brother…" he wheezed, unable to catch his breath.

"Why would you feed me information if you were only going to kill me?"

"Not… trying… to kill… you… just…" George struggled for air.

Red snapped up a playing card- a one-eyed jack of all things- and went to his brother. He ripped open George's shirt and wiped the frothy pink blood from the wound. He covered the hole with the playing card and grabbing George's hand, pressed it to his chest.

"Hold that there tight and lean over. Better?"

George caught his breath and nodded, but the color was rapidly draining from his face.

"Are you the head of Section Eleven?"

George's eyes grew wider, realizing his brother had played him, drawn him out. He shook his head and attempted another deep breath.

"I'm run field intelligence analysis, upper management. The wing command is my cover."

"So you're not pulling all the strings, just sorting them out for someone else to yank on. Were you ordered to kill me? Or just slow me down?"

"When we found out about the vault under the Sheriff's house, the order came down to take you out by any means necessary. They gave me the job."

"How Shakespearean of them," Red twisted his lip into a smirk. "You didn't know about the vault, did you? Your goon squad burned the Sheriff's house to the ground, hoping to destroy any evidence of Hoyle's involvement in whatever black ops bullshit y'all had going on."

George nodded. "The whole thing caught us by surprise. We had written off Lee years ago."

"Jefferson Lee, killed in action, ten years ago," the question was implied.

"Lee volunteered…" George paused to catch his breath "… to go to the other side. But when he came back… he was changed. Different. We couldn't control him. He wiped out most of the unit in less than five minutes."

"Other side… other side of what?" Red asked.

"Best you don't know."

"Again, why feed me information if you were ordered to kill me?"

"Because you're my brother," George grabbed Red's hand and squeezed it tight. "You… I had hoped you could expose this mess before I ran out of excuses." George peeled the playing card back from the hole in his chest. A fresh river of blood flowed from the wound. "I just ran out of time."

George grimaced, clenching his teeth, his face bone white. His limp hand fell away from Red's.

George was dead.

16:32

Red stood in a phone booth, muttering a quiet prayer for strength and forgiveness. He dialed his sister-in-law's phone number, when she picked up, Red almost hung up. Somehow though, he found the ability to speak.

"Eloise, this is Red... Jack, I need..."

"Jack! I was just trying to call you! George got home last night not even ten minutes after we spoke. He knew you'd be looking for him and he feels terrible about it, but he had to go to overseas for a month or so, some air force thing again. I never know with him. He gets called away every few months to deal with a special project or some other secret mission. I won't hear from him again until he walks through the front door."

Red didn't know whether to be glad for the reprieve or furious about George's foresight. It took all of Red's effort to maintain some sense of composure and maintain a light tone with his widowed sister-in-law.

"Did George say anything other than he was going out of town?"

"No, not really. He did say to tell you he loved you very much and that he was sorry."

Red thanked her and wished her well, promising to come by for dinner in a few days. He hung up and stepped out of the phone booth into the sunlight. The tears burned his eyes before Red could wipe them away.

The respite wouldn't last forever and there were still too many questions, not enough answers. He wasn't sure if the cost of pursuing this was worth it. His devotion to justice was unimpeachable but there comes a time in such futile endeavors to cut bait and move on.

If he could meet these clowns on neutral ground, maybe he could convince them that he was done...

Every minute swept away by the hands of the clock did nothing but strengthen the urge to do so in this case. This afternoon, the death of his only brother had him teetering on the edge.

He could run to the South Pacific again.

Like he did after Angie killed herself.

Run like a coward.

Red slid into the Ford he had borrowed from Cactus Jack, contemplating which way to go when a man opened the passenger door and jumped in side.

"Drive. Now."

Red began to protest but he noticed the man had a pistol in his lap, trained on Red. He dropped the truck in gear and pulled onto the road.

"Where are we going, friend?"

"East. Take the highway." The man kept looking in the side-view mirror. Red checked the rearview mirror, but saw no tail. Five miles down the road, the stranger told Red to turn off onto a state road. After another mile, he motioned Red to take a rutted trail across a pasture towards a copse of trees.

The man never took his finger off the trigger.

Red never bothered with any attempt at small talk.

Red parked in a clearing amongst some post oak and shut down the engine. The man in the passenger seat sat for minute, listening for any unnatural sounds out in the woods, checking the trees for any prying eyes. The only sounds they heard were a few birds and the ticking of the V8 as it cooled. Satisfied they were alone the man motioned for Red to get out of the cab.

Together they walked another hundred yards into the thicket. Parked at a crossroads in the trail was another car, a '47 Chevy Stylemaster.

"Keys are in the ignition. Follow this trail for about half a mile and turn right. After another mile, you'll get to a farm road. Go left and you'll eventually hit the interstate. Go south and get to Houston as fast as you can. They're moving on Lucas Brown and you need to get him first."

"Who the hell are you?"

"I'm a friend of your brother. We worked for the same group but we both shared the same... disillusionment with their authority. He said if I didn't hear from him by three o'clock this afternoon to find you and get your ass to Houston as quickly as possible. Now, get going. Time is wasting."

"You're his contact with Section Eleven, one of the two men who flew with him to the Russian border. According to George, you helped found the group. Why aren't you trying to kill me like everyone else?"

The man was getting agitated the questions, but he decided to answer, "No, I'm not him. I was just an operator, nothing more than a grunt, but I had been there since the beginning. Now I'm retired, as of three weeks ago. From what I hear, Ben Hoyle had my obituary tacked to the corkboard, down in his bat-cave..."

"Frank Unger, eaten by a tiger."

"This organization is one you never truly leave, not even when you're dead. Eventually they will find me out and they will make that fake obituary a reality. I could tell you a tale or two but there is no time. You have to get to Lucas Brown. He can tell you where to find Tony Paxton. He's the real key to blowing this mess wide open but three days ago, he vanished without a trace. Section Eleven can't even find him. That scares the hell out of *everyone*. Now get in that car and get your ass to Houston."

"What is this Section Eleven playing at? What is so damned important about a murdered sheriff and an escaped POW?"

The exasperated man grunted and looked at his watch.

"Did George not tell you who it was that held Lee in captivity for the last ten years?"

"I assumed it was either the Russians or maybe the Chinese..."

"'There are more things in heaven and earth, Horatio, than are dreamt of in your philosophy.'"

"What the hell is that supposed to mean?"

The man just smiled, but it was dry, tired smile. He just shook Red's hand, wished him good luck and walked away, whistling a piece from Faust.

Red didn't know what to think of the man, so he climbed into the Stylemaster and turned the key. As he pulled away, he watched the man vanish into the forest through the rearview mirror.

He never saw the man again.

At least, not in this world...

Even as the Stylemaster chewed through the farm roads and highways with ease, Red couldn't help but think he was going to be too late. The sky was turning crimson as the sun was slipping and he could see lights of the refineries on the edge of southeastern horizon, twinkling to life in the gloaming twilight. With the windows rolled down, he could smell the distinct odor of sulphur on the gulf breeze blowing in across Texas City and Pasadena.

He hated coming to Houston.

The sedan slid to a stop in front of the Gulf Building, on the corner of Capitol and Main Street. Red jumped from the car, hurrying inside. The offices had closed at five pm, but as the wheels of modern industry know no time clock, many people were still coming and going an hour after quitting time.

The directory in the lobby indicated Brown Coastal and Refining occupied the top four floors- a far cry from the warehouse Lucas Brown was working out of when Red first met the man three years ago. A doorman tried to stop him but the Ranger kept on moving through the lobby into the elevators. Mashing the button for the top, Red patiently waited for the car to ascend the 34 floors.

Red stepped into the BC&R lobby, immediately dropping into a crouch. He could see a pair of very fine looking legs laid out on the floor behind the reception desk in a most unnatural manner. He crept to the woman, and was relieved to find her only unconscious. She had a nasty bruise on her temple but her breathing was normal and her color good. Red lightly smacked the woman's cheek, but the best he could get out her was a slight moan. She had been in the process of leaving when her assailants jumped her. A purse was on the floor next to her crumpled coat and a set of keys were clutched loosely in her hand. Red folded the coat around the purse and put the bundle under the woman's head. It was the best he could do for her at the moment.

He found a set of stairs and sprinted to the top floor, Lucas Brown's office would be up there somewhere. Carefully cracking the stairwell door open just an inch, Red quietly listened for a moment. Down the hall, on the west side of the building, he could hear shouts and random gunfire.

It sounded like a standoff.

In the back of his mind, he wondered why he couldn't hear the fighting before exiting the stairs...

Drawing his 1911, Red checked the magazine and the chamber- seven plus one. With the two extra mags in his back pocket, he had a total twenty two rounds. Easily more than enough, he thought to himself, stalking towards the firefight.

The former roughneck's office occupied the southwest corner of the thirty-seventh floor. There was only one door in and one door out. In his personal secretary's office, three men in bad suits were trying to shoot their way in to Brown-Section Eleven.

They were barricaded behind a heavy wooden desk, taking pot shots with revolvers. Every time one of them tried to make a move, a shotgun blast would erupt from the darkened doorway leading into Brown's office. Sprays of buckshot and flying chunks of mahogany kept the group from advancing. Two bodies already lie motionless between the upturned furniture and the door to the inner office, Luke was taking no prisoners. Red could hear him shouting from the darkened room...

"You bastards seriously think you're going to take me down? '*Disappear*' me? I am Lucas Mother Fucking Brown! I turned down the CMH for killing bastards more worthy of dying than you! You should have brought more than five guys to take me down, you wannabe secret squirrel motherfuckers! When I'm done with you sons of bitches, I'll take a drive out to Iron Mesa and kill every god *BOOM!* damned *BOOM!* last *BOOM!* one of you!"

Two more rounds of double-aught-Buck tore through the room, but in the deafening silence following the barrage, everyone could hear the audible click of the twelve gauge dry-firing.

Luke Brown was empty.

As the last three attackers jumped up, Red came around the corner, gun raised, ready to put the men down. But the oilman stepped out of the shadows of the office, carrying a Browning automatic rifle, laughing like a kid on Christmas morning.

The Ranger dove for cover just as Brown opened up. The spooks were blown to pieces by a hail of .30-06 slugs. Blood and gore splattered the room, covering everything. Lucas Brown was red from head to toe, smiling like a mad dog killer, a fat cigar clamped between his teeth. Its aromatic smoke mingled with the stench of gunpowder and death swirling in the air.

"Anybody else want some?"

Red slowly stepped out from around the corner, both hands raised. He could see Luke's finger tightening on the trigger. The oilman relaxed when he recognized the Texas Ranger.

"'Bout goddamn time you got here, Captain Jack. I called you down here on Monday."

Red lowered his hands, hooking his thumbs in his belt, surveying the carnage. "Sorry, sarge, something came up."

The oilman slung the BAR over his shoulder and took the cigar out of his mouth. He was about to speak when the lights went out, plunging the interior office into darkness. Red instinctively drew his weapon.

"We need to get out of here. Now."

"No arguments there, Jack."

Before the men could move for the stairs, all the windows looking out of Luke Brown's corner office exploded inward, raining glass across the dark grey carpet. Luke spun around, bringing his BAR to bear. Red assumed a fighting stance just outside the room but he couldn't get a clear line of fire into the office- the oilman stood in the way and the setting sun was shining right through into the Rangers eyes.

All he could make out beyond Brown's stout frame was a figure in black silhouetted by the sun, standing on the giant oak desk in the center of the room.

"You…" Luke whispered to the figure that towered over the room as if an angel passing judgment. Red could smell the fear rolling off the man- the burly ex-sergeant soiled himself.

The figure in black spread his arms out in front of him, fingers outstretched like the talons of some great bird of prey. Cold blue flames licked from the man's fingertips, coalescing in his palms before shooting to the ceiling like arcs of electricity, exploding all the sprinklers overhead. A sheet of water cascaded down over everything in the office.

Lucas Brown, soaked in blood, water and his own filth, began to visibly tremble and shake. The BAR slipped from his hands, his arms pulling in towards his chest. His fists balled up so tight, Red swore he saw blood streaming from in between the fingers. Incredibly, unbelievably, the man assumed a fetal position, floating in midair, faintly glowing with a purple sheen as the water continued to rain down from the ceiling. Luke made a thin keening through his clenched teeth that soon crescendoed into a

156

howling wail, the shaking of his body becoming more violent.

And suddenly, with an audible *pop!* the man was gone.

Red only waited half a second before his jaw snapped shut and he emptied eight rounds of forty-five auto into the man standing on the desk. But the figure in black just laughed, leaping backwards out the window as the hot slugs punched through his chest. Reloading as he ran through the broken glass, Red was intent upon emptying another seven rounds into the man as he fell to street, nearly four hundred feet below.

To Red's shock and dismay, the man survived another hail of bullets and the fall. Instead of splattering across the sidewalk upon hitting the pavement, the man just got up, nonchalantly dusted himself off and walked into the shadows. As he disappeared from sight, his laughter hung in the air like the sulphur stink of the refineries to the south.

Red hated coming to Houston.

Thursday
August 18, 1955

07:13

To Red, stepping off the DC-7 at Moisant Field was like stepping into a wet wall of cotton. It wasn't even eight o'clock but the needle on the thermometer was already tickling ninety degrees. There wasn't a cloud in the sky, but the humidity was already well over eighty percent. Within minutes, Red's shirt was stuck to his back and he was in no good mood.

Last night, before the smoke could clear and the bodies had gone cold, Red had left Houston as fast as he could. The continued acts of breaking protocol and committing what were without a doubt gross derelictions of duty gnawed at the Ranger's guts. He had never abandoned a crime scene before this investigation, but it couldn't be helped anymore. As he had watched the man in black walk away from fifteen gunshots to the chest *and* a four hundred foot fall, three black sedans pulled up on the sidewalk below, more agents from Section Eleven, no doubt. Red slipped out of the building unseen.

He had rented a motel room up on the north side of town, but he was only able to grab an hour or two of fitful sleep. The image of Lucas Brown vanishing into thin air was seared into his mind, the sound he had made still echoed in the Ranger's ear. He had finally given up on sleep and left behind the sweat soaked sheets, catching the early morning flight to New Orleans.

He followed the other passengers across the tarmac to the bland hanger that served as the airport's terminal, trying his best to blend into the crowd. In place of his customary Stetson, Red wore a brown fedora and tan seersucker suit. His badge was shoved deep in his pocket and his guns were tucked in his bag, out of sight but certainly not out of his mind. Dark sunglasses covered his eyes as they scanned the sparse crowd for any signs of Section Eleven.

This early in the morning, there weren't many people in the terminal. Red had to dodge the one random family of tourists meandering around the information booth- they sounded Dutch and completely lost. The other dozen or so travelers appeared to be businessmen, indifferent to the comings and goings of the other people, focusing on making a connecting flight or finding a cup of coffee. There was no sign of any government agent anywhere to be seen.

Red stopped off in the men's room, splashing some cold water on his face. The man scowling back at him in the mirror was a bit haggard. He

couldn't remember the last time he shaved –
Tuesday night? The black circles under his eyes
betrayed the lack of sleep that had accumulated
since then. It would be nice to lie down in a
comfortable bed for a good eight hours. That
would have to wait.

Red slipped his sunglasses back over his
bloodshot eyes, straightened his tie, squaring
himself away.

Nothing to do but to get to it.

Out in front of the terminal the Ranger
grabbed a cab, telling the driver to take him to
Jackson Square. He figured a beignet and a cup
of coffee from the Café du Monde could only
help.

After two plates of beignets and nearly a pot of coffee, Red felt more or less human again. He was able to sweet talk his waitress into bringing him the café's phone book- Anthony Paxton's office was on Magazine Street, just outside the French Quarter. His home address was over in the Garden District. The Ranger decided to go by the office first. If the lawyer had any staff, they might have some information to share.

But before he did anything, Red rented a room at one of the nicer hotels on Bourbon Street. The king sized bed was very tempting, as was the big soaking tub, but the only luxury he took was a shave. He strapped his guns on and pinned his badge to his vest. The Ranger checked himself in the full length mirror, the shoulder holsters barely showed through the seersucker jacket. It was not his normal uniform, but Red figured it best if he didn't really stand out in a crowd. A Ranger was supposed to be dressed in western attire when on the job, but this investigation had gone off the reservation days ago. A cowboy walking around the French Quarter would draw all the wrong kinds of attention.

He dropped his fedora on his head and stepped out.

Instead of taking a cab, the Ranger walked the few blocks to the law offices of Paxton and Bonnechere. The Quarter was just starting to come to life, as much as it ever could this early on a Thursday morning. Trucks delivered fresh cases of liquor to the bars as sweepers cleared the sidewalks of last night's debauchery. The aroma that hung in the air was not too terribly unpleasant- the smell of garbage and the muddy Mississippi River flowing four blocks away was relentless, but the steam of roasting coffee beans and the homeliness of baking bread made it tolerable.

It was a complex odor, textured in a way that was almost visible to the Ranger's naked eye.

He arrived at Paxton's office and tried the door, but it was locked. He knocked, waiting for a few moments, but he saw no signs of life. He was about to jimmy the door when a woman finally answered.

She was a slim, exquisite mulatto, probably thirty or so years of age. She wore a white shirt and a grey flannel skirt. Her eyes were puffy and red, the tracks of her tears plainly visible, as was the three day old bruise on her left cheek.

Red pretended not to notice the gun she held in her hand, hidden behind her back.

"I am Captain Jack Horne, Texas Ranger. I'm looking for Anthony Paxton."

"I haven't seen or heard from Tony since Monday morning."

"It's imperative that I find him. Do you know where he might have gone?"

"No, I don't. Now please leave."

"Ma'am, I only have a couple of questions and then I will be on my way."

162

The woman set her jaw and cocked the hammer back on the revolver, but did not show the weapon. "I am not a ma'am, I am a miss. Ask your questions quickly and be on your way."

"We should talk inside."

The woman stood her ground, "Right here is just fine."

Red had never been on this side of that kind of threat.

He didn't much like it.

"What set Mr. Paxton off? What gave him reason to walk away and just disappear? Something must have spooked him, and I'm guessing it had something to do with the murder of Ben Hoyle?"

"He came in Monday morning and read the phone messages before I could go through them. He took them with him when he left, but I had copies sent over from the service." She handed Red a slip of paper.

The message simply said Ben Hoyle had passed. The time stamp was a blazing red flag, seven o'clock, Sunday morning, not fifteen minutes after Hoyle's sister found her brother dead at her door. Who sent the message, Red could only guess. There was no indication on the slip of paper.

"Mr. Paxton and Ben Hoyle served together in the same unit during the war. Do you know if they have any kind of relationship afterwards? Did they keep in touch?"

"One week out of the year, Tony would disappear into the bayou with his war buddies.

163

Ben Hoyle was one of them. There were two other regulars, Luke Brown and Eddie Cork." Red was not at all surprised by her disgusted shiver when she uttered the dead doctor's name. "Sometimes, a couple of other guys would fly in from overseas, somewhere in Europe or maybe Asia. I don't remember their names."

"Do you know where he goes out in the bayou? Is it a regular spot?"

She had no idea where he went out there, but she was sure he had mentioned a fishing camp somewhere amongst the maze of canals west of Dulac, near Hackberry Lake maybe, but the exact location, she didn't know.

Finding a fish camp out in the bayou would be next to impossible.

"Who else has come by asking questions about Mr. Paxton?"

"New Orleans Police have been by, once, on Tuesday morning. But the officer didn't do much more than scratch doodles in his little notebook. He left without making any kind of assurances to look for Tony. After all, he left willingly and wasn't under any kind of duress."

"Is the police officer the one who put that bruise on your face?"

The woman lower lip trembled almost imperceptibly. Her hand went to cheek, covering the blemish on her face. Red just noticed the brilliant rock on her finger, sparkling in the morning sunshine. She recovered quickly however, her brow furrowing with intense fury.

"No, sir. That was put there by the other men, the ones who came by Monday afternoon."

"Did they appear to be military, possibly government agents?"

The woman nodded. "The police were about as concerned with the assault complaint as they were about Tony going missing."

"How long have you and Tony been engaged?"

The woman blushed, ever so slightly.

"Three months. The wedding was supposed to be September first."

"Miss..?"

"Bonnechere, Cordelia..."

"Miss Bonnechere, I will do my absolute best to find your fiancé. I cannot promise any more than that. I won't sugar coat it, there is danger for everyone even remotely involved in this mess. As a precaution," Red took a business card from his wallet and wrote a number on the back. "This is my sister's phone number. I want you to pack a few things and go out of town for a few days. When you get to where you're going, call Kate and give her a number that I can reach you at."

"I have relatives up in..." Red cut her off before she could finish.

"Don't tell me where. Just go. I check in with my sister every other day. When I find Tony, I will give her a call and we'll go from there."

"*When* you find him?"

"I will, Miss Bonnechere. One way or the other, I will find him."

Red tipped his hat and turned to go. He paused on the last step, turning back to the lawyer's fiancée.

"One last question, how good are you with that gun you've got hidden behind your back?"

Cordelia smiled, whipping the firearm around without hesitation, blasting three pigeons off the roof line across the street and knocking two more out of the air.

"Good enough," Red smiled.

Paxton's home was in the Garden District, on the corner of Fourth and Prytania Street, a two-story affair with a large front porch, situated on a large lot surrounded by a black wrought iron fence. The house appeared empty but Red decided on prudence. He walked around the block a couple of times before going in through the back.

The door was ajar, the frame a splintered mess. Red gingerly pushed it open and stepped inside.

Every room was in disarray, furniture overturned, cushions and pillows slashed, drawers opened and their contents strewn across the floor. It looked like a burglary, but the Ranger knew better. Section Eleven had come and gone.

After a quick survey throughout the house, Red came to the conclusion that he wouldn't find anything of use to him. The lawyer seemed to have lived a Spartan life to begin with, but whoever had tossed the place had removed any vestige of personality that might have existed. There was not a single shred of paper left in the house, none. The drawers and filing cabinets in the lawyer's home office were emptied, even the picture frames were smashed, the photographs removed.

Red went out the front door and sat down on the front steps, elbows on his knees, fingers laced together, his chin resting on his thumbs, deep in thought. As he sat contemplating his next move, a shadow fell across the steps.

"You the Texas Ranger?"

Red looked up at the two men. Both wore New Orleans PD uniforms. If they knew to find him out here, he wondered where the Section Eleven spooks were watching from. Red was found that he didn't even really care at this point.

"I'm Sergeant Dilley, this is Patrolman Forchette. Would you mind coming with us?"

"Where are we going?"

"Our captain would like to speak with you down at the division headquarters," Forchette spoke up, hand resting on the butt of his service revolver.

"About?"

"Jurisdictional courtesies."

Red stood and wiped the seat of his pants. "Lead the way."

10:19

Division headquarters was on the corner of Tulane Avenue and South Broad Street, an imposing structure, with the words 'Law' and 'Order' emblazoned high and mighty on either side of the Broad Street entrance. Along the top of the building, high above the door was a chiseled a powerful phrase, off hand Red couldn't recall if it was a direct quote or a paraphrasing of the words of John Adams:

This is a Government of Law Not of Men

Red had held strong to that philosophy, kept it dear in his heart ever since he swore that oath to uphold and defend the Constitution, but he was starting to doubt the power of those words when considered in the context of the current reality...

The two officers led the Ranger inside, through a maze of desks to a cluster of offices. No one appeared to be paying attention to the group, but it was obvious everyone was interested. It was not every day a Texas Ranger was escorted through the building. If Red had asked for a show of hands, he'd have found the feelings were about fifty percent awe, forty percent fear, and ten percent contempt. This was Louisiana, after all, and the rivalry between them and Texas was long and storied, much deeper than a college football game.

The Division Chief's office was on the second floor, behind an unmarked door. Sergeant Dilley kept an eye on Red while Patrolman Forchette knocked on the frosted glass.

"Bring him in here," a voice growled from inside. Forchette opened the door and waved Red through. The Ranger didn't bother to remove his hat as he stepped inside.

Captain Paul Mosier stood by the window with his arms across his barrel chest, his back to the room.

"It is common courtesy for visiting law enforcement agents to let their counterparts know when they intend to conduct an investigation within their jurisdiction." The captain turned to face the Ranger. "But you don't waste time on common courtesies, do you? You breeze into town without so much as a 'howdy do' and then proceed to wreck the joint."

"It's what I do best. You ought to remember that, Master Chief."

The captain stepped around the desk, standing toe to toe with the Ranger. The two men glared at each other, Red had a good six inches on the captain, but Mosier was built like a fireplug and looked like he had chewed barbed wire and drank gasoline for breakfast every single morning of his fifty three years. The office space seemed to be getting smaller by the second as the Ranger and the Captain squared off, toe to toe. Neither man flinched. Patrolman Forchette began to say something, but his sergeant muttered for him to keep his mouth shut.

"Good Lord, you are still one ugly son of bitch," Red said.

"When you get to be my age you won't look half as good," the captain replied. For a moment, the men coolly stared into each other's eyes, neither willing to give an inch. The impasse broke with a sudden fierce bear hug, each man slapping the other on the back, laughing generously. Forchette was completely baffled. Dilley just watched with mild amusement.

"Gentlemen, meet Commander Andrew Jackson Horne, the best damned naval officer I ever had the pleasure of serving with."

"It's Captain, now," Red pointed to the shield on his breast.

"Well now, how do you do, Captain?" Mosier acknowledged with profuse and excessive flourish, bowing low.

"Captain," Red returned the flourish, both men chuckling like morons. Sergeant Dilley pushed Forchette out the door, closing it behind him.

"How have you been, Red? I haven't seen you in damn near six years," Mosier offered Red the chair across from the desk. The chief took two cigars from a box on the corner of his desk, handing one of the rich, dark brown maduros to the Ranger. He lit a cedar spill with his Zippo and held the light for the Ranger.

"Oh, I've been alright, making my way through," Red puffed the cigar, coughing hard after the first pull. "What the hell is this?"

"It's a local brand, good for you, puts hair on your chest."

Red puffed on the cigar, once he got past the first draw, it was pretty damned good, strong and earthy, but with a hint of sweetness.

"I gotta ask, how did your boys know to find me this morning?"

Mosier flipped a business card across the desk, "Big bird came by Tuesday morning, and said a man claiming to be a Texas Ranger would be poking around sometime over the next few days and to keep an eye out."

Red didn't recognize the name on the card- S.A. Krosier, Colonel, USAF. "What else did this guy say?"

"He might have mentioned that we should shoot you on sight."

"Well, I thank you for not doing so."

"Yeah, I told my boys that if they saw a man with a red handlebar mustache and a shifty look in his eye to bring him in. Good thing you didn't take my advice and shave that God awful thing."

Red just grinned behind the 'stache, twirling one end.

"So what's up with the flyboy?" Mosier asked.

"He and I are looking for the same thing, an attorney."

"They don't have any in Texas?"

"This one was a war hero, goes by the name Paxton."

Mosier leaned forward and flipped through the box of business cards by his phone, "Anthony Paxton, Esquire. I've met him a few times down at the court house, a right tenacious bastard, regardless of which side he's arguing, kind of a prick, but an honest and fair prick. A lot like you. What's he done to pique the interest of the Texas Rangers?"

"He's been missing since Monday morning."

"Huh. Hold on a minute," the captain toggled a speaker on his desk. "Forchette, check and see if we have a missing persons file on an Anthony Paxton. Bring it in here if you find it." Mosier sat back in his chair, hands clasped behind his head, puffing on his cigar. "Missing since Monday... If your flyboy friend came by Tuesday, they must not have found him."

Forchette opened the door and handed a thin manila folder to the Captain. Mosier told him to wait a minute as he flipped the file open.

"This is bigger than a missing person's case, isn't it?" the Chief asked, flipping through the flimsy stack of papers.

"He's a material witness in a murder investigation."

"Well, that certainly changes things. Who got himself killed?"

"The sheriff of Hoyle County, a man named Ben Hoyle. He and Paxton were in the same unit during the war. When Paxton got the message that Hoyle was dead, he hauled ass."

"Now that's hardly more than a coincidence, Red. How does that make him a material witness?"

"Well, the day after Hoyle had a hole burned through his face, a man named Ed Cork had his throat slit in a VA hospital. Another man, Lucas Brown, was…" Red paused for a second, still trying to rationalize the events from last night, "well, he's gone missing as well. With those three gone, Tony Paxton is the last surviving member of a covert special ops unit that made a run into Soviet Russia back in '45. My best information tells me they left behind one of their own and now he's come back. The last man on his list is hiding out in a bayou somewhere."

"What does the Air Force want with him, the lawyer?"

"They want to keep him quiet about whatever it was they did over in Siberia. When the man they left for dead showed up, it must have kicked off something big. And I don't think this Krosier is actually Air Force."

Mosier closed the file and snapped his fingers for Forchette's attention.

"Go find Sergeant Theriot. I want him in front of my desk, ten minutes ago." Forchette sprinted from the office, not bothering to close the door behind him.

"This," Mosier spun the file across the desk, "is garbage. No mention of a message or a dead sheriff, just a statement that the man walked into his office Monday morning and walked right back out." Mosier mashed the intercom on his desk. "Where the hell is Sergeant Theriot?" A muffled voice squawked back some unintelligible gibberish just as Theriot was ushered in by Forchette. Mosier shouted for the patrolman to leave and commenced to dressing down the sergeant.

"Sergeant Theriot, you transferred here from Baton Rouge, what… two weeks ago?"

The man fidgeted a bit, not knowing what to expect.

"Yes, sir. The wife and I moved in with her parents, they're getting on in years."

"Right now, I could give shit about your in-laws. What I want is for you to explain this," Mosier threw the report at his sergeant. The man tried to catch it, but the few pieces of paper fell to the floor. He scrambled to pick them up.

"There wasn't anything to it. That lawyer fellow walked in, read a note, and left! The nig…"

Mosier shot up from his chair, cutting the sergeant off with the back of his hand. "Use that word again and you'll be mucking out of the mounted division's stables every goddamned day from now on until your retirement." Red never moved from his chair, enjoying the show. He hadn't realized until just now how much he had missed the Master Chief.

"Stand at attention, you!" Mosier barked. The sergeant snapped to, his face beet red. "You sorry sack of mule piss! After two weeks, you should know by now how things are done in this division, *my* division. I only demand two things: respect for the law and respect for the citizens, REGARDLESS of race or creed. Now, you're going to go back to see Miss Cordelia Bonnechere," Mosier got right up in the sergeant's face, nose to nose, "You're going to apologize for being an incompetent, insensitive, ineffective jackass. You're going to beg her forgiveness for your complacency. Then you're going to interview her again and you're going to rewrite this piece of trash," Mosier ripped the papers from the sergeant's hand, tearing them in half and shoving the pieces in the man's shirt pocket. "And I want it in my hand by one o'clock. Oh, and along with the revised report, I want a five-paragraph essay on why I shouldn't take you out in the street and beat some respect into with my bare hands."

"Today?" the sergeant asked.

"Yes today, goddamn it! Now get out of my sight!"

The sergeant saluted and turned on his heel, exiting as quickly as he could. The officers out in the bull pen quickly turned their attention back to their phones and their own reports, attempting to look busy and uninterested. Mosier slammed the door shut and turned to Red.

"Sorry about that. These guys... sometimes I could just..." Mosier looked to the ceiling, shaking his fist, growling to God for strength of mind and personal restraint. He sat down hard behind his desk, the chair protesting loudly. He uttered an apology to the framed picture standing on his desk next to his phone- a faded photograph of him and his wife on their wedding day, some thirty years ago. "I know I promised I wouldn't let that crap get to me anymore, Peka, but I'll be damned if I can let it slide."

He looked back to Red, shaking his head.

"Goddamn it was so much easier back in the day."

"If it were any easier, it wouldn't be any fun, now would it?"

Mosier snorted. "No, I guess it wouldn't." The Chief leaned back in his chair, lacing his fingers together over his chest, "So, what else do you know about this mess? Your suspect, they left him for dead, you say?"

"I'm not entirely sure of what happened over there. He was either left for dead or was captured by enemy forces, Russians maybe. I'm assuming the colonel that dropped by here is part of the heavy duty intelligence group that ran the mission."

Mosier took the cigar from his mouth and spit a bit of tobacco leaf from his mouth in contempt. "I'm betting that you've had a run in or two with these clowns already."

"Yeah, several times now. They burned my house to the ground and are indirectly responsible for the death of my brother."

"I'm sorry to hear about George. I hope you dealt with them accordingly."

Red tapped the butt of his gun. "An appropriate level of response has been applied. But as always, they have the numbers on their side. I keep stacking them up like cord wood, but there's only so much one man can do by himself. And the suspect- all I've got on him is a name and evidence that he has access some sort of weapon that can burn a hole clean through body, a perfect three inch diameter. Oh, and the fun part- anyone shot with it eventually turns into a block of ice. Paxton is the last man alive who can tell me what went down on that last mission. I need to find him, ASAP. According to his fiancée, he might be hiding out in the bayou somewhere. I don't even know where to begin looking for that needle in a haystack."

"Why, Captain, are you asking for help?"

"I usually don't have any qualms asking for it, but over these last few days, some of the people I've asked a favor from have met with some pretty severe consequences. And the shit storm will probably just get worse, regardless of whether or not I find Paxton and a few answers. So, Master Chief, as much as it pains me to do so, yes, I need your help."

Mosier got up from behind his desk and walked around to Red, offering his hand. The Ranger stood, accepting the handshake.

"To Hell with all that bullshit, all you had to do was ask," Mosier grinned around his cigar. He threw open the door and hollered for Patrolman Forchette. When he came into the office, Forchette was surprised Mosier offered him one of his smokes.

"How do you like your job, Danny?"

"I love my job, sir. Serving and protecting the people of…"

"Serve and protect, yeah, yeah, yeah," Mosier cut him off. "You hate being stuck in the office behind a desk, don't you? You despise being my personal bitch."

Forchette shot a quick glance at the Ranger, but Red shook his head.

"Don't look at me."

Forchette turned back to the Chief. "I want to be out on the streets, where the action is. I didn't join the force to be a damned secretary."

"When you married my only daughter six months ago, that's exactly what you signed up for." Red didn't like where this was going, but he kept his mouth shut. He'd trusted Mosier explicitly and without question when the two men were serving together. He had no reason to doubt the man's judgment now.

"I'm taking a few days off to help my friend with an investigation. In spite of what you and the other men in this precinct think, I am not bulletproof, nor am I immortal. There was a time me and Red here could take on an entire battalion by ourselves. Hell, that's exactly what we've done a time or two. And we've got the scars to prove it. But truth of the matter is, I'm getting old. I need someone I can trust to have mine and Red's backs when we get to where we're going. I need someone well grounded and absolutely cool under fire. This is your chance to get back out in the field."

Forchette studied the cigar in his hand, sliding it under his nose, inhaling the earthy aroma. He bit the end off and took a light from the Captain.

"When do we leave?"

"Twenty minutes. Go change into your civvies and meet us in the motor pool."

Forchette gave Mosier a salute and headed out. Red closed the door and turned to his old chief.

"I can't guarantee that kid will live to see Sunday morning."

Mosier pulled a bag from under his desk and checked its contents. "Don't worry about Danny Boy. He may be family, but he's also an ex-Army Ranger. Two tours in Korea. He's seen a lot of the same kind of Hell we've seen, if not worse. I only stuck him on desk duty as a favor to my daughter. He'll do alright. Hell, the kid will probably show us a thing or two."

"If you vouch for him, I won't worry about it, but... *Army*? Damn, Chief, I thought you had higher standards than that."

"When your daughter falls head over heels in love, there's not much you can do about who it is."

16:04

The drive from New Orleans to Dulac took a little over two hours. Red sat in the back seat, hat pulled down low over his eyes, catching a nap. Mosier sat up front, reading a dime western while Danny Forchette drove the car.

They didn't leave New Orleans until well after lunch, almost one thirty. Mosier was adamant about getting an updated report from Sergeant Theriot before they headed out. And the cafeteria at the courthouse had some of the best crawfish etouffee in town.

It was also a good place to troll for information.

Paxton was well known in the courts. He wasn't an employee of the District Attorney's Office, but when he wasn't defending against them, he would work a case for them on occasion. Rumor was a run for the office was around the corner, but a lot of Paxton's contemporaries didn't think the lawyer would actually do it. He too much fun trying cases in the courtroom to be stuck in a management position.

One of the clerks they spoke to remembered Paxton mentioning his annual trip out into the swamps. The clerk remembered because of the colorful description Paxton gave of the charter captain he used every year- a ninety-some-odd year old Creole named Ramses du Fontaine. Whether or not Fontaine had ferried the man out to the bayou Monday morning, they'd find out soon enough.

The sedan pulled up in front of the docks, crunching through the sun-bleached shells of the parking lot. When Red stepped out of the air conditioned car, he was pleasantly surprised by the breeze- it had been hot and sticky in New Orleans, but by the time they reached Dulac a brisk wind was blowing in from the coast and he could tell the barometer had started dropping.

The skies were still mostly clear and blue but a few ragged clouds were drifting in from the Gulf. Red popped the trunk of the car, thinking it was nice weather for a few days trip into the swamp.

While Danny gave Red a hand with unloading the gear, Mosier was arguing with a withered old man occupying a rocking chair that looked as ancient as him. Red couldn't tell if the man was black, white or Indian- he'd never met a true Creole before. Decades of living and working under the Gulf Coast sun had turned his skin into a wrinkled leather hide. The old boat captain never bothered to remove the bare-assed Pall Mall from his lips as he dickered with Mosier about a charter.

"He wants three hundred dollars to take us out to where Paxton *might* be," Mosier spat as Red and Danny walked over.

"I can drive a boat for three hundred dollars," Danny growled. The old man cackled with glee.

"Hell, you can drive de boat fo' free but you noah never fine de man you lookin fo', chere,"

Ramses du Fontaine rocked back and forth in his chair. Red wasn't sure if it was the chair creaking or the old man's bones.

"Three hundred is pretty damned steep," Red crossed his arms, studying the docks behind the boat captain. Three airboats were pulled up on the grass by the water's edge and a couple of small shrimpers were tied to the weathered pier. A few private boats were riding the tide in rented slips. He'd never piloted an airboat, but he knew his way around a skiff pretty damned well. "Did Paxton actually come through here in the last few days?"

"He come tru Monday round noon. He rented a boat, drove himself out in to de bayou. If you want t' rent a boat, de price is fifty a day. If you want a guide, tree hund'd is my going rate. A hund'd to get out dere and a hund'd to get back. De other hund'd is fo' the trouble."

"But you can't guarantee that Paxton will be there."

"Oh, I jess bout guarantee he is where he is. I can noah guarantee you make it to where he is."

"Why is that?" Mosier demanded, clearly agitated with the imp and his rocking chair.

"Hurricane be a coming." The old man pointed south, over Mosier's shoulder. Danny shook his head.

"Weatherman said nothing about a hurricane."

Ramses spit on the ground and laughed. "De weather man is a fool an' a half, chere. De hurricane it be here in t'ree days. We leave tomorrow mornin' or we doan leave at all."

"Four hundred and we leave in an hour," Red pulled a wad of cash out of his pocket, peeling off four bills. Ramses laughed hysterically as he snatched the money from the Ranger's hand. He finally took the cigarette from between his lips, whistling over his shoulder. Two young men—twins about seventeen years of age came out of the boat house.

"Romulus, Remus, gas up number five an' load a pirogue. Den takes dees boys to Vouvia Bayou." Ramses lit another cigarette, ignoring Mosier's displeasure at arrangement.

"I can't believe we're going to have a couple of kids taking us out into a goddamn swamp, at night."

"My boys know des waters better than any man tree times dere age. Dey born out dere. Dey live out dere. Dey goan die out dere someday. An' dere kids goan do de same."

Mosier rolled his eyes and went to help Danny load the gear into the boat.

Red turned back to Ramses.

"Has anyone else been out here looking for Paxton?"

"No, chere. You de first. I'm guessing you woan be de last."

Red peeled another four hundred dollars of his bank roll.

"There will probably be another group of men coming along after us, looking for the same thing we are. This is to take them the other way."

Ramses looked at Red hard in the eye and took the money.

"Easy t' get turned 'round in de bayou. Real easy to get et by de gator, too."

"Just keep 'em occupied until your boys bring us back, but if you want to have a little fun with them, by all means," Red gave the old man a sly wink and turned to help with Danny and Mosier with the rest of the load out.

The old Creole kept rocking his chair back and forth, cackling now and again with laughter.

Easy money.

The crew pulled out of the docks an hour before sunset, heading southwest, deep into Terrebonne Parish, Mosier complaining constantly about starting out this late in the day.

The Master Chief was born and raised in Louisiana, but he had spent his youth prowling the streets of New Orleans, only venturing out into the swamps for the occasional hunting trip with his grandfather. The idea of sleeping in a hammock suspended over gator infested waters brought back some childhood memories Mosier did not relish revisiting.

Red didn't give a damn one way or the other. He shouldn't have had the need to remind the Chief about the two years they spent together, island hopping through the south Pacific, playing hide and seek in hothouse jungles while gathering intelligence and generally gumming up the works of the enemy forces. And when compared to the horror of four months in a Japanese prison camp, a night in a hammock out in the bayou was a week at the Ritz.

"Come on Red, you ought to know I'm not happy unless I'm bitching about something. That's Master Chief 101."

About the only thing Mosier didn't bitch about was Romulus du Fontaine. It only took about five miles for the old master chief to become massively impressed with the kid's nautical skills, hardly believing he was only seventeen. Romulus knew every canal and cypress knee like the back of his hand. The airboat glided through the marsh with precision. About half an hour after sunset and almost ten miles into the swamp, the kid beached the airboat on the one piece of real dry land they'd come across since setting out.

The island wasn't that big, maybe half an acre, the highest point three feet above the water. Red could make out the remains of a house, silhouetted by the dying sunset. It wasn't much more than an outline of tumbled bricks and the remnants of a stone chimney leaning drunkenly to one side, but it was obvious that people still used the place. A chord of firewood was stacked neatly under a tin lean-to, built against a lightning blasted oak. Within the ring that was once the homestead's outer wall a few pallets had been laid out around a fire pit. While the men set up their tents, Romulus got a fire going.

"This was once a whole town, but then the levee broke, flooding everything, about thirty years before I was born," Romulus volunteered. "Pop grew up out here. In fact, this used to be his house. He never comes out here anymore. My brother and I use this place if we get caught out here after dark. Or if we just want to get away from the old man."

"How much farther is it to Paxton's camp?" Danny asked, absentmindedly chewing on a piece of beef jerky.

"About four hours. We'll have to use the pirogue for the last two miles. It's best to go slow and quiet in that area."

Red took his boots off, hanging them upside down on a pair of sticks he'd planted in the turf, just inside his tent. "If we leave out of here at dawn, we should make it to Paxton's camp well before noon."

"If the weather holds out," Mosier muttered. "I think that old coot was right. More clouds are moving in. I would not be at all surprised if we get soaked tomorrow."

After a quick meal of dried pork and a few cigars, Danny, the Chief and the kid crawled into their tents and were soon fast asleep.

Not feeling at all tired, Red sat staring into the flames, reflecting on the past few days.

He'd put nine men in their graves, including his own brother. The sheriff and his wife were murdered, a surgeon dead by his own hand, an oil executive literally vanishing into thin air right in front of Red's own two eyes, and a lawyer hiding somewhere out here in the swamps...

And the vengeful ghost of a man left for dead ten years ago was running loose, blowing holes through people.

Red finally gave in to fatigue. Hopefully the lawyer could answer some questions tomorrow. He crawled into his tent, not bothering with the sleeping bag. As he drifted off to sleep, Red seriously considered finding another line of work when this case was done.

Friday

5:03

Red was awakened by a firm hand on his shoulder. It was still a half hour before sunrise and it was raining.

It was the kid, Romulus. His face was set like stone, but his eyes telegraphed pure terror. He held out something in his trembling hand, urging Red to take it.

"Put this on, now, and keep quiet until I come get you" the kid whispered before withdrawing from the tent.

It was a small medicine bag on a leather cord. Red had seen these before, a totem meant to ward off evil spirits. He had never believed in their magic, but his cousins did. And the fear in Romulus' eyes was convincing enough. Red slipped it over his neck without hesitation.

Through the damp leather, he could smell camphor and sulphur.

Red tried peering through the open flap of the tent, but the low clouds and misty rain made the light of pre-dawn grayer than usual. The canvas door of the tent severely limited his field of vision as it slowly flapped opened and shut

189

with the breeze. He could just hear Romulus waking Mosier, giving him a medicine bag as well, but after that he heard not a sound.

Nothing at all.

There should have been frogs croaking and crickets chirping, all manner of swamp critter chattering as the day was about to begin. But Red only heard the falling rain, tattooing the canvas overhead.

Then, a twig snapped, giving Red's strained senses a focal point. He bent his ears, listening hard for another sound... a footstep fell, directly across the clearing, near the lean-to and the dead oak tree. He studied the stump and the pile of firewood, ticking off the seconds, cursing the timidity of the rising sun and the gray curtain of raindrops, but Red saw nothing moving.

There, by the dead tree trunk, something moved, maybe. But Red's eyes told him nothing was there. Red used sheer willpower to pierce the gloom between him and the six foot tree stump. As his eyes adjusted to the miniscule contrast between light and shadow, a cold hand crept up through his guts. It was nothing, Red told himself; just a trick of the light making the blasted oak look like it had a face. But then what Red thought only looked like a man made out of wood stepped away from the tree and out of his field of view.

It was only a brief second in which the Ranger saw the thing moving, but that second would be etched in his mind, a snapshot forever burned into his memory, unforgotten even beyond the bounds of his natural life.

The thing had unfolded from the tree trunk like a great insect, standing a foot taller than the burnt trunk. Its arms and legs were spindly, knotted but with a smooth texture, like well-worn wood. The torso was twisted, like a thick jungle vine, deeply furrowed, lumpy in all the wrong places. Its face... God if Red could forget that face he'd never ask for anything in prayer ever again.

The head was misshapen, but roughly human. The eyes were nothing more than empty black sockets. The nose was missing, as was the upper jaw and cheek bones, making for a gaping ragged maw, studded along the bottom with a few rotted stumps that might have once been teeth. Red would swear the thing had been looking right at him before stepping away from the tree stump and stalking off.

Red felt as if his soul might collapse in on itself. He had looked Death in the face many, many times, witnessed all the varied and grisly horrors the human race could dream up and perpetrate against one another, but this thing... this was not of this world.

What was worse, Red could hear several of them walking through the camp, unnatural steps making their way to the water's edge. He could hear them stepping into the lake, casually splashing through the black water, heading out into deeper water.

Ten agonizing minutes later, the frogs started up again.

Mosier was the first to move. He exploded from his tent, knocking it down as he leapt into the clearing, his Winchester Model 94 held in a vise-like grip. He yanked Romulus up by his collar, practically head-butting the kid.

"What in the name of Jesus H. Christ was that thing?" he hoarsely whispered. Danny came out of his tent and got between his father-in-law and the kid. Red yanked his boots on and checked his pistols.

"Those were guardians. They're not supposed to be this far out."

"Guardians? Guardians of what, exactly?"

"Our sacred grounds, where the lawyer is hiding with some of our people." The kid was already moving, throwing gear into the pirogue they had brought out with them.

"If they're the guardians of *your* sacred grounds, why the totems?" Red asked as he pitched his pack into the airboat. The kid grabbed the bag and threw it into the pirogue instead.

"No airboat. We have to go silently now. The guardians don't come out in the daylight, but they can move about underwater. They don't care who you are, Creole or white devil. They will drag you down into the black mud and make you one of them. The totems help to make us invisible, but the guardians key off movement and they are surprisingly fast. They can take a man down in a heartbeat."

"Horseshit," spat the Chief. "Pure horseshit. Next you'll tell us Bigfoot is their captain and the Jersey Devil their King."

192

"The skunk ape fears the guardians. And I don't know what the Jersey Devil is," Romulus grabbed a pole and stepped into the pirogue. "We have to go. *NOW*. Back to Dulac."

Red shook his head. "No, we have to get to Paxton."

The kid, clearly scared out of his mind was doing his best to hide it.

"You said they're not supposed to be this far out. Why would they be?" Danny asked.

"I don't know. I've never heard of them coming west of Hellhole Lake. Something has drawn them here."

"Drawn them or drove them?" Red asked, looking at the clouds overhead. It was looking like the hurricane would be here a lot sooner than 'tree' days. "I'll pay you an extra two hundred to take us the rest of the way."

Romulus shook his head. "What good is money if I'm walking the earth for the rest of eternity as a guardian? We're going back to Dulac."

"Okay then, how about two hundred to rent the airboat and you show us on the map where we're going?"

"A thousand for the boat and directions."

Mosier was about to ring the kid's neck when Danny stopped him again. "A thousand? Are you out of your goddamn mind?"

"A thousand to buy the boat. I'll only sell it to you because I know I'll never see it again and my father will take it out of my ass if I don't come back with something."

"Fine," Red replied, pulling his wallet out of his back pocket. All he had was eight hundred. "You guys have any cash?"

The Chief threw his hands up in the air and stormed off. Danny dug deep, producing a fifty and five twenties, "That's all I've got."

Red handed Romulus the money and the kid shoved it deep in his jeans pocket. He tossed Red's pack on the wet grass and shoved off.

"Wait a goddamn minute! You didn't tell where we're supposed to go!"

"You only paid me nine fifty. You're all sailors. You've got a map. Vouvia Bayou is that way," he pointed west. With one good shove, the kid disappeared into the falling rain.

"Now what the fuck do we do?" Danny growled, throwing his backpack in the airboat.

"Like he said we have a map and a compass, what the hell else do we need?" Red started taking down his tent.

"A goddamn psychiatrist, that's what!" Mosier shouted from across the camp, throwing his poncho over his shoulders. "I don't know if you saw it, but a goddamn *tree* walked right through here and into the water. Now, that Romulus is only a kid, a damn child, but he's lived out here his whole damned life. And if he's scared shitless of those things, then we should probably follow him back to town."

"If it moves around on two legs that means it's alive. And if it's alive, that means it can die," Red slung his guns over his shoulders, "and you know I am damn good at killing things."

"Fine then," the Chief grumbled. "Let's get the hell out of here before we drown."

The light of the sun could not penetrate the heavy clouds, keeping the bayou in a perpetual gloom. The rain fell sideways, driven by steadily increasing winds. Stronger gusts buffeted the boat and the occasional heavy squall dumped gallons of water on the men, forcing them to take turns with the constant bailing.

It was slow going.

They didn't use the engine on the airboat until they were at least a mile from the island, instead using poles to move the flat-bottomed craft quietly through the black water and cypress. But the farther they got from their encounter with the guardians, the less they believed it really happened. When they hit open water, they fired up the engine, making their way across the lake as best they could.

Hugging the southern shoreline, they bounced over the slight chop. If they kept the wind to their backs, it wasn't too bad, but more than once, the Chief managed to nearly dump the boat as he steered around a floating log or drifting sand bar. He ignored the glares from Danny and Red, concentrating on the throttle, rudder and the waves. All the Ranger and Dan could do was hang on for dear life.

They beached the boat just before entering Bay Voisin, taking a break to check the map and make a wild-assed guess as to where the lawyer might be.

Sacred grounds weren't usually marked on a grid and waterways had a way of shifting in the bayou, but according to the map, Red and Mosier figured their best bet would be to continue west into Bay Voisin, cut north into King Lake and then cross Mudhole Bay. When they hit Junop, they would make a straight run down to Hellhole Bay and then on to Big Hellhole Lake. From there, it was due west to Vouvia Bayou.

The Chief had been a blue water sailor before signing up as a frogman. Red had spent a lot of time fishing the rivers of west Texas while growing up. For most of his naval career, he had been a commando, never actually driving a boat. They both thought a direct course the best. But the only one with any experience in the swamps soon talked them out of it.

Danny had grown up in Lake Charles and had spent more than a few weekends cruising through the Atchafalaya river basin. He knew enough to override the Ranger and his father-in-law's navigational decision. But, as he confidently made his case, he was silently wishing to himself the du Fontaine kid hadn't abandoned them...

They had several problems, the most serious of which was the chop on open water. The shallow draft airboat just wasn't made for it. With the strengthening winds and increasingly heavy rains, the likelihood of being capsized or swamped was more than certain. By the time they reached King Lake, it would be too rough to safely make a run straight across. They would have to navigate smaller canals where they could, sheltering the boat from the brunt of the wind amongst the trees. A better, safer route would be to follow a secondary canal around Bay Banan and Indian Bay into Taylor's Bayou. If they skirted the south end of Bay Junop, hugging the shore as they did with Caillou Lake, they could more safely make their way through to Hellhole and on to Vouvia Bayou.

The Chief and Red looked at the skies and the water, realizing their haste to find Paxton had kept them from recognizing the obvious. Mosier was a little put out that an Army grunt had shown him up on the water, but more than anything he was angry with himself for completely ignoring the obvious. Grumbling to himself, the Chief climbed into the pilot's seat and hit the ignition switch…

Nothing happened.

Mosier held his poncho over the motor, spewing one random explicative after another while Red and Danny checked the fuel and electric lines. They couldn't find anything wrong with it until the Chief pointed to the distributor cap. A widening crack ran along one side, allowing water to get in. When Red tried popping the cap off, the plastic broke in half and a chunk of it fell away. Too many years outside in the sun had made the plastic material too brittle to handle.

"That's just... fucking fantastic," growled the Chief.

"Looks like we're paddling the rest of the way," Red tossed the two halves of the distributor in the bottom of the boat. He and Danny grabbed their poles and started pushing the boat along.

It was going to be a long day.

12:07

The rain actually began to let up as the sun climbed towards its zenith. Ragged blue skies tore through the clouds and things began to dry out a bit. But the three men in the boat knew the break in the weather was only a brief window of opportunity. Looking southwest, they could see another wall of clouds, the top of which was just peeking over the horizon.

They dried out the halves of the distributor cap, hoping they could somehow make it work, wrapping it together with a piece of leather strapping after setting it down over the points and condenser. The engine ran for all of ten minutes, but it got them that much further along.

At this point, they were just entering King Lake. They took turns pushing the boat along with the long poles in the shallows and rowing with the paddles when the water was too deep. The winds were still brisk, blowing from the east southeast, but the chop had subsided enough to risk the more direct route across open water. They made good time to the entrance of Bay Banan. Pressing on, they made Taylor's Bayou by one thirty, but instead of following the bayou south into the wind, they cut north into Cross Bayou, scooting across Bay Junop.

They landed the boat at the mouth of
Hellhole Bayou just as the winds were picking
up and the rain moved in again. They tried using
the canvas from one of the pup tents to shelter
themselves in the boat, but the violent gusts
made it a pointless endeavor. The rain was
blowing sideways again, soaking everything.
Red and the Chief gave up, huddling in the boat
under their ponchos, waiting for another break
in the clouds. Danny didn't think it was going let
again, not for a good long while. With a
disgusted grunt, he stepped out onto the shore
and headed for the bushes.

"Don't go too far, Dan," the Chief advised
his son-in-law. Danny just waved a hand over
his shoulder and kept on walking.

"Must need to take a shit."

"Probably should have just hung his ass over
the side of the boat," Red opined. "Got any dry
smokes?"

"Hell no."

The two men sat in silence for about ten
minutes. The wind was pushing fifty knots
sustained, the drops of water stung like Hell. It
was miserable and it was only going to get
worse.

Ramses du Fontaine had been right. The
weatherman was a fool.

The drumming rain on the aluminum hull
had just about lulled Red to sleep when Danny

came sprinting back to the boat. He leapt over the side and grabbed his shotgun. Mosier raised his rifle, Red drew his 1911s.

"What is it?"

"There is something out there. I think it's those things from this morning."

"Bullshit. It's just a gator."

"In this kind of weather? You know as well as I do they're all hiding out on the bottom. Something was walking through the bushes on two legs. And I heard it sniffing."

"Sniffing?" The incredulity in Mosier's voice was unmistakable. "How can you hear sniffing in this wind and rain?"

Danny scanned the edge of the bushes. There wasn't much of a beach, just three feet of sand between the water and the waist high vegetation. He suddenly put his shotgun down and grabbed a pole, shoving the boat into the water, away from land.

"Whoa! What are you doing? The boat's filling up with water faster than we can bail!" Red grabbed the pole from Danny, but the man just yanked it back, pointing to a gnarly log sticking up out of the foliage about fifteen yards to the east of where they had been beached.

"That was not there when we landed."

Red looked and realized Danny was right. Then the dead tree moved.

The guardians were back.

The creature wasn't alone. A second had popped up from the bushes where Danny had gone exploring. A third was standing about thirty yards to the west- all three were sniffing the air. Red could hear it now, a hollow gravely sound. He let go of Danny's pole and grabbed the other one, shoving hard to distance the boat from the shore. Mosier began bailing water as fast he could without making a lot of noise. How these creatures could hear anything above the howling wind and the pounding rain, Red had no idea.

But somehow they did.

The one on the port side began advancing at a steady walk, directly towards the boat. The one to the fore zeroed in on them as well, high stepping over the bushes as it came. The one to the starboard side just walked straight into the water, disappearing beneath the surface.

Muttering curses under his breath, Danny put the pole down and grabbed his shotgun again. Mosier dropped the bailing bucket, picking up his Winchester. The guardian in the middle began to lope, sprinting the last ten yards to the water's edge. It leapt into the air arms spread wide, a demon bird spawned from Satan's worst nightmare. Danny blasted it in half, his pump-action 10 gauge booming like a canon. Mosier put five rounds of 30-30 through the one still on the beach, blowing its head to smithereens.

"Sons of bitches *can* die!" Mosier shouted above the hurricane.

"Keep it down!" Red barked at the Chief, "There's still one more out there!" The Ranger kept pushing the boat away from the beach, away from where the third guardian had gone into the water, struggling against the wind and the current. Mosier quickly reloaded as Danny kept an eye on the water. The wind was getting stronger, in a matter of minutes it had gone from fifty to at least seventy knots. With gusts nearing ninety, Danny was having a hell of time staying on his feet as he swept the surface of the water with his Remington. Visibility was less than forty yards and it was impossible to see below the water's surface.

Red kept pushing with the pole, trying to turn the boat back towards the shore, but it was getting harder. And the water was only getting deeper as the storm surge moved in. Soon, there would be no land to walk on for miles.

The Ranger pulled the pole up, readying to push one more time when it was ripped from his hands. Even as slick with rain as it was, the wooden shaft laid open Red's palms, ripping the flesh away. The Chief stood and emptied five rounds into the water as fast as he could, working the lever action rifle like a machine gun.

"Do you think I got it?" Mosier shouted to Red.

"Probably not. That was a fifteen foot pole; I was barely reaching the bottom."

"It's screwing with us," Danny shouted, wiping the water from his eyes with his sleeve, a useless gesture. He pointed the big ten gauge at the lake. "I hate the goddamn water."

"We're thirty feet from the shore line. We can make it to land," Mosier yelled, pointing to the beach. The Chief was ready to swim for it. Having been dropped in shark infested waters more than once, he was willing to take his chances. Red grabbed his sleeve and held him the boat.

"The wind is driving us to the other side of the channel! Just wait for it."

"Yeah, dad. Just wait for it," Danny shouted.

"You said it yourself, son, this thing is fucking with us! If we can get it up on the beach we can blow the goddamn thing to Kingdom Come!"

From below the boat, there was a tremendous thump, jarring the three men to silence, knocking Mosier off his feet, flat on his back in the bottom of the boat. Danny sat down hard on the forward bench.

"It's under us," Danny mouthed through the howling wind. A second lighter tap on the hull was followed by an explosion of blinding lightning and deafening thunder- the bolt from above struck a cypress tree not more than a hundred feet from the boat. When the purple-white glare faded from their vision seconds later, they saw that the guardian had shoved the pole through the bottom of the boat and Paul Mosier.

Impaled through the heart, the Chief was dead.

Danny began to tremble and shake, his screams drowned by the fury of the storm. He unleashed his own with the shotgun, peppering the water with round after round. When the ten gauge was empty, Danny picked up his father-in-law's Winchester and fired into wind whipped water. When that was empty, Danny went for his service revolver, but the boat shuddered beneath their feet. Red and Danny suddenly found themselves flying through the air as the guardian flipped the vessel from under them. They hit the water and immediately struck out for the shore, know not ten feet away.

They were clawing at the mud bank when Danny let out a shriek of terror, piercing the cacophony of the hurricane like a sonic drill bit. Red turned just in time to see the man dragged under the water by the last guardian.

The Ranger pulled his guns and screamed for Danny, but it was useless. A minute went by and the water continued to rise. Red kicked himself backwards, up to the brush line, guns trained on the water, waiting for the guardian to come forth and claim him as the grand prize. The second hand swept through another half minute, Red clenched his jaw tight, grinding his teeth flat. When the surface of the water finally erupted like a fountain, the Ranger very nearly unloaded all sixteen rounds into the spray, but he checked himself just in time. It was Danny.

And he was alive.

Red dragged the man from the water up into the brush. They collapsed in the mud and wind and rain.

"What the hell happened? I thought you were dead!"

"I don't know. I was able to get my gun and shoot the damn thing but it wouldn't die. It kept tightening its grip, dragging me deeper and then... it just let go and swam away. Something scared it off."

"What in the name of God could scare one of those things?"

"Well, let's not wait around to find out."

The two men struggled through the deepening water towards the tree line they'd spotted before the blinding rains had come back. It was at least a hundred yards away and soon they'd be swimming. The last guardian was still out there, maybe even more of them. And though they had seen none all day, this was still a Louisiana swamp and there were still gators out here somewhere.

The plan was to get to one of the massive cypress and climb it, lashing themselves in the branches, as high as they could get, and wait out the storm. The two struggled through the fading light, not able to see more than ten feet in front of them, praying they were still heading in the right direction when they found themselves surrounded.

Several boats had come, gliding out of the wet gray hell, three massive vessels that seemed to defy the storm. Powerful searchlights found the Ranger and his companion. Red held a hand up in front of his eyes, trying to block out the glare.

A voice called out over a loudspeaker...

"Jackson Horne, you're a long way from Texas."

Red tried to see who was speaking, but he could only see globs of shadows behind the lights. "I'm looking for a lawyer."

"A lawyer? Out in this mess? Most people run the other way from an attorney."

"He's a material witness to a murder investigation." Out of the corner of his eye, he noticed Danny had his weapon in his hand, low down by his side. Red caught the man's attention, nodding towards the revolver and shaking his head 'no'. Danny shoved the gun in its holster, the damn thing was empty anyways.

"You're a right tenacious bastard, coming out here in the middle of a hurricane to question a witness. What useful information do you think this lawyer might have?"

"I need to know what happened to Jefferson Lee during Operation Water Park. I need to know why he's killing everyone he served with on that mission. Most of all, I need to know why you're scared of him, Mr. Paxton."

The loudspeaker went silent for a moment as Red and Danny waited in the rising water. Then the search lights were doused and the lead boat came closer. Several arms reached over the gunwale, lifting Red and Danny out of the water. They were disarmed and lead into the wheelhouse.

The interior of the cabin was rigged for general quarters- red lamps behind wire cages burned bright as the crew ignored their stations, intently watching Red and Danny as they stood quietly dripping water on the deck.

Tony Paxton, looking almost exactly as he had in the picture Red had found on the dead sheriff, sat in the pilot's chair, his feet propped up the console. He lit the pipe clamped between his teeth, shaking out the match, tossing it into a butt kit. He looked the Ranger and the police officer up and down with an intense, piercing gaze.

"You boys look like a couple of drowned rats," he spoke around his pipe. He turned to his first mate, "Don't they, Sam?"

The Choctaw chuckled. "Like a couple of nutria running from a gator."

Red looked the lawyer up and down as well, noticing the lawyer was missing his right arm above the elbow. Paxton caught him looking and waggled the stump his way.

"I suppose you want to know how I lost this."

"The thought never crossed my mind," the Ranger lied.

"Well, if you want to know what happened to Jeff Lee and why he wants kill every last god forsaken son of a bitch he ever knew, you'll find out where my arm went." The lawyer planted his feet on the deck and shoved the throttle over, the boat's twin diesels lurching against the hurricane outside.

"Welcome to Hell, boys."

The story continues in

Jackson Red Horne

Volume Two

The Hammer of Hephaestus

About the Author

J. K. Hulon

J.K. grew up all over the great state of Texas, from Cut and Shoot to Carrizo Springs and just about everywhere in between.

Following a tour of duty as a military police officer at Naval Support Activity Agnano, Italy, J.K. pursued work in various fields: retail loss prevention, register jockey, prison guard, punk band roadie, electrical coil winder, audio board operator, and television news photographer to name but a few.
Currently, he earns a paycheck watching sitcoms, old movies, and cartoons, preparing them for on-demand distribution.

In addition to writing, J.K. enjoys photography, shooting his forty-five semi-automatics, and smoking a fine cigar while sipping whiskey.

J.K. resides in the Atlanta area with his wife, two cats, and a Ford F-150 named Francene.

15360050R00125

Made in the USA
Charleston, SC
30 October 2012